PUFFIN BOOKS

THE BOYFRIEND WARS

"You're not talented," Roni yelled. "And you don't have the personality to be a star."

"You really have nerve," I said. "If that's the way you feel, forget about having me for a campaign manager. You'll find out who's got personality when you have to run against me."

"You're going to run against *me* for president?" Roni snorted. "You really think you stand a chance?"

"I can tell you one person who thinks I'll make a good class president," I said.

"Who is it – one of the nerds? Or someone who needs new glasses?"

"Neither," I said smoothly. "It's Josh White. You know, the guy you like? He's volunteered to be my campaign manager."

Janet Quin-Harkin was born in Bath and educated in England, Austria and Germany. She studied dance and drama as a child and went straight from college to work for the BBC, where she wrote several plays.

Yearning for sunshine she went to Australia to work for Australian Broadcasting. Within weeks she was given a contract to draw a daily cartoon for the *Australian* newspaper. In Sydney she met her husband. The Quin-Harkins moved to California, where they lived for twenty years and raised four children.

Janet Quin-Harkin began writing children's books when living in San Francisco. Her first picture book, *Peter Penny's Dance*, won many awards, including *The New York Times* Best Book of the Year Award. She has subsequently written more than fifty books for young adults.

Janet Quin-Harkin is now a full-time writer and also teaches creative writing at a nearby college.

The Boyfriend Wars

.Also available in the Boyfriend Club series

the boyfriend club

11

The Boyfriend Wars

JANET QUIN-HARKIN

PUFFIN BOOKS

PUFFIN BOOKS

Published by the Penguin Group
Penguin Books Ltd, 27 Wrights Lane, London W8 5TZ, England
Penguin Books USA Inc., 375 Hudson Street, New York, New York 10014, USA
Penguin Books Australia Ltd, Ringwood, Victoria, Australia
Penguin Books Canada Ltd, 10 Alcorn Avenue, Toronto, Ontario, Canada M4V 3B2
Penguin Books (NZ) Ltd, 182–190 Wairau Road, Auckland 10, New Zealand

Penguin Books Ltd, Registered Offices: Harmondsworth, Middlesex, England

First published in the USA by Troll Associates Inc. 1995
Published in Puffin Books 1995
1 3 5 7 9 10 8 6 4 2

Copyright © Janet Quin-Harkin and Daniel Weiss Associates, Inc., 1995
All rights reserved

Produced by Daniel Weiss Associates, Inc.
33 West 17th Street, New York, NY 10011, USA

The moral right of the author has been asserted

Made and printed in England by Clays Ltd, St Ives plc

Prologue

GINGER HARTMAN. HER DIARY. KEEP OUT.
HARTMAN FARM, SOMEWHERE IN THE BOONIES
NEAR LUBBOCK, TEXAS
AUGUST 2ND

Dear Diary,

I've been here a week now, and that's too long! I am dying of boredom and mosquito bites. We're staying with Uncle Elmer on his farm—Dad's idea, not mine. Uncle Elmer had some sort of heart surgery, so Dad kindly volunteered us to help out with the chores. Nice of him, huh? It's okay for my brother Todd, because he gets to drive the tractor. But I'm supposed to help with the household chores and yucky stuff like feeding chickens. Chickens are scary birds. I nearly got pecked to death the first day here. They have such beady little eyes. I think they're really aliens plotting to take over the planet.

It doesn't matter which way you look from the farmhouse, all you can see is flat nothing. Even if there was something to do, I wouldn't want to do it with my dumb cousins anyway. They are so annoying. Talk about juvenile. The first night here they put a frog in my bed—that's their idea of fun. I'd expect that kind of behavior from the boys—they're only kids, after all. But my cousin Lacey is my age! She should know better. She's such a wacko! She goes around saying things like "Gol-lee," and "Holy cow," and she makes fun of me because I can't tote bales of hay. Why on earth would I want to know how to do something like that? Then she asks all these stupid questions about life in the big city and how many dates I've had. (I've only ever dated Ben, but I'm tempted to make up some glamorous boyfriends to keep her happy.)

I'm actually praying for school to hurry up and start again. Can you believe it? Only four more weeks now. I can't wait to get back to civilization and my friends and Ben. I bet my friends are having a fun summer with no farm chores. If only I played the violin, maybe I would have gotten a scholarship like

Karen to that fancy music camp in the mountains. I bet Roni's having a great time with her cute cousins in Mexico. I can just imagine Justine in her itsy-bitsy bikini on the beach in San Diego, pretending to drown so that the lifeguards can rescue her. I'm dying to see them all again. Imagine—we'll be sophomores!

Shoot, as Lacey would say, gotta go. I have to help shuck some corn. Hee-haw!

WHAT I DID DURING MY SUMMER VACATION
BY RONI RUIZ

(*I'm writing this now, while it's all fresh in my mind, in case it really is an assignment in English—then I'll be one step ahead of everybody!*)

Mexico is hot, dry, and dusty, and nothing ever happens. I guess plenty of stuff happens in Acapulco or even Mexico City, but not in the little town where my grandmother lives. I have had enough of family togetherness for the rest of my life! I'm fed up with speaking Spanish all the time. I know I speak it to my mom at home, but it's not the language I think in anymore, or dream in, or feel in.

Every day some relative comes to visit and I have to be hugged and pinched and asked a zillion questions about my life in America. I wish I could be living my life in America right now! Girls my age down here have sweethearts, and they can only go out with a chaperon. It's very primitive. "Sweethearts," that's what they call them—isn't that funny? Drew would've laughed if I'd told him he was my sweetheart. Of course, he isn't really, anymore. . . . But if I had a sweetheart, he'd look a lot like Drew. Not like those boring, sincere Mexican boys my relatives keep introducing me to. They are so obvious it's hard to believe. I can't wait to get back home to Ginger and my friends and yes—even back to school!

I'm too tired to write any more. It's too hot. Siesta time!

KAREN NGUYEN. DIARY.
HIGH CREST MUSIC CAMP, COLORADO ROCKIES
AUGUST 3RD

My fourth week here. Two more weeks to go. I guess I've learned a lot. One of the things I've learned is that musicians are very boring people. All they want to talk about is music. And the other students are so dedicated. Most of them actually want to practice four or five hours a day. My instructor told me

I'm very gifted and if only I practiced more, I could think ahead to the concert stage. I'm flattered, but I wish he'd said that I was a klutz who didn't have a chance. I just don't see myself as a violinist all my life.

It's very beautiful up here. Lots of aspens and pines and bubbling streams. The air smells wonderfully fresh. I'd like to go for long walks through the woods, but we never have time between rehearsals. And there's another reason I wouldn't want to go out for a long walk alone—Jeremy might follow me. I'm sure he's harmless enough, but boy, does he bug me. I didn't ask him to develop an instant crush on me. I wish he hadn't. One of the good things about going home to Phoenix will be no more Jeremy staring at me with a dumb grin on his face or hanging around my cabin like he did last night. The other good thing will be seeing Ginger, Roni, and Justine again. I really miss them!

JUSTINE CRAFT. JOURNAL OF INTIMATE THOUGHTS.
PRIVATE.
BEACH HOUSE, LA JOLLA, CALIFORNIA

Dear Diary,
    It's another glorious, sunny day. I can't decide

what to do—should I talk to that cute lifeguard again, or go shopping in the boutiques of downtown La Jolla, or pester my stepmother about taking me over to Tijuana? I bet Ginger and Roni and Karen wish they could be having a fun-filled, sun-filled summer like me. It was a great idea of Daddy's to rent the house so that Christine could have a relaxing summer with Alexandra while he's away in England on business. My new sister really likes me (actually I think she likes me best, but I keep quiet about that). I call her Alex. It suits her better. She's turning into a real person now, and she smiles and wriggles when she sees me. I love it.

If only I had some friends my own age to do stuff with, it would be perfect here. It's mostly older rich people. There's one totally cute lifeguard named Larry. I've tried flirting with him, I've tried bringing him cold drinks, I even tried a fake drowning once, but he just smiles and says hi and that's it. It's like he doesn't even notice I exist. Is the guy blind or what? How could he resist a gorgeous blonde like me?

We go home next week. I'm not looking forward to school starting and harder classes and homework, but I can't wait to see my friends. I need a new boyfriend, too. Better go clothes shopping today so that I start with a new, cute wardrobe. Ciao.

Chapter

1

"Will you relax?" Roni said. "You're running around like a chicken with no head."

"They'll be here any minute!" I said. "And don't mention chickens to me. I've had enough of chickens to last me a lifetime." I gave the pillows on my bed a final plumping. "Do you know what time roosters crow?" I demanded. "I'll tell you. They start at three A.M. Right outside my window. I didn't sleep for a month."

Roni laughed. "Tell me about it! We had roosters in Mexico—and donkeys who liked to hee-haw at the top of their voices. And scorpions in the bathroom. I guess you're not a fan of the simple life either."

"You can say that again," I answered, shuddering.

"Give me civilization, dishwashers, and air-conditioned malls any day."

"Right on," Roni said. "Not to mention fast food and MTV—and no relatives that kiss you!"

"Not even those cute cousins we met?" I teased.

Roni made a face. "The cute cousins weren't there," she said. "They live in Mexico City, five hundred miles away. This was just my grandmother, ancient great-aunts, and second cousins twice removed who kept kissing me and pinching my cheek and telling me it was about time I got married."

I had to laugh at her grossed-out face. "Poor Roni! Your summer sounds as bad as mine."

"Worse."

"At least we're fellow sufferers," I said. "Any second now we'll have Karen and Justine telling us all about their fabulous time at the snobby, upscale places they've been."

"Karen would never brag," Roni said quickly, "and it was really amazing that she won that scholarship. You know she had to be good to be picked from thousands of applicants."

"She *is* good," I said. "She sounds like a professional to me. I wonder if she's more enthusiastic about her violin now. I always got the feeling she didn't like it as much as her parents did."

Roni nodded. "I'm dying to find out," she said. "And of course we know Justine will have to boast about everything—her mansion on the beach and her great tan and all those California hunks she's met." She looked up at me. "I'm never sure why we like her, really."

I laughed. "Sometimes I ask myself the same thing. She can be a pain sometimes, but she's generous, too. She's always lending us clothes or treating us to things we couldn't afford. And you have to admit she's funny."

"She doesn't mean to be, but she is," Roni agreed. "I suppose we might have turned out like Justine if we'd been to all those snobby boarding schools instead of good old Oak Creek Junior High."

At the mention of Oak Creek, we both made gagging noises. Neither of us could think of junior high without getting hives. Thank goodness we weren't *there* anymore!

"I wish they'd hurry up and get here," I said, still pacing nervously. "Does my room look okay? Do you think I should make some popcorn, or will the brownies and ice cream be enough?"

Roni grabbed me by the shoulders and shook me. "Ginger, it's only Karen and Justine who are coming, not President and Mrs. Clinton and Chelsea! They know what your room's like. They've slept over here a zillion times, for pete's sake."

I smiled. "I know," I said. "I'm just so excited that we're finally getting together again that I want everything to be perfect."

"It's as perfect as it's going to get, without rushing to the mall and buying a whole new bedroom set," Roni said, looking at my beat-up old furniture. "Face it, your room's never going to look like Justine's, but who cares? We like it here. Your dad never bugs us and your brother's hardly ever around. It's perfect for a sleepover."

I put a hand on Roni's shoulder. "Thanks, best friend," I said. "I don't know what's gotten into me. Actually, I *do* know—it was three weeks of my cousin Lacey. She's enough to turn anyone into a nervous wreck. If she was here now, she'd be asking me if I shouldn't put new covers on the pillows and shampoo that yucky spot out of the rug and maybe run myself up a new dress on the sewing machine and pop a few loaves of corn bread into the oven."

"Sounds like a pain," Roni agreed.

"Total pain," I said. "And she laughed when the chickens attacked me. I'll never forgive her for that. She said, 'Shoot, Ginger, you ain't scared of a few little bitty birds, are ya?'"

"The chickens attacked you?" Roni asked with a grin.

"They were big, fierce chickens and I fell over backward into their feed dish and they climbed all over me. It wasn't funny," I added when I saw her mouth starting to twitch.

"Sorry," she said. "Well, you're home now and Lacey and the chickens can fade away like a bad dream."

"And we can start planning for school," I said. "I never thought I'd hear myself say this, but I can't wait for school to start."

"Me neither," Roni said. "Imagine us—sophomores. Little freshmen will have to get out of our way in the halls. They'll tremble when we look at them. We'll know our way around, we'll be cool and confident, smart and sassy." She flung out an arm and hit my lamp. "Whoops," she yelled as she grabbed it in midair and righted it again.

I smiled. Roni would never change. She'd always be loud and dramatic, full of energy and fun. I was so glad to be back with her again—we'd been best friends ever since kindergarten. It was strange to be away from her even for a few days. Of course, we'd had our fights, but we'd always been there for each other. Now we had Karen and Justine, too, and we did everything with them, but Roni and I were still best friends.

The sound of car tires scrunching on gravel made us both jump.

"They're here," Roni shouted. We fought each other to get to the front door first. I won. I'm used to competing with older brothers, so I'm better at shoving.

Justine's stepmother stopped her baby-blue Mercedes in the driveway. Justine, looking more tanned and gorgeous than ever, her blond hair bleached almost white, was unloading bags from the front seat. She was wearing a white lacy top, tied above her waist to show a bare, tanned midriff, and a tiny pair of white shorts with a big sunflower embroidered on the back pocket.

"Pop the trunk," she yelled to her stepmother. "I've got more stuff in there."

Roni and I glanced at each other, then at the heap of stuff that was already beside the car.

"That's our girl," Roni muttered.

"Hi, Justine," we yelled, running down the path to the car.

"Hi!" she screamed as she hugged us in delight. "Sorry we're late, but I couldn't find the pillow that matches my sleeping bag. Don't you just adore these shorts? I got them in this fabulous boutique in La Jolla. You should have seen the lifeguards' faces when I wore them on the beach. . . ."

Karen climbed out of the backseat, smiling at us shyly.

"Karen!" Roni yelled, and enveloped her in a big hug. I ran to join in.

"Hi, you guys. I sure missed you," she said, beaming with pleasure.

"Someone come and help me lift this out," Justine commanded from the trunk.

I grabbed a huge overstuffed sports bag and swung it out easily.

"Wow, what muscles," Justine commented. "I guess all that farm work paid off, huh?"

"Don't talk to me about farm work," I said. "What have you got in here? It weighs a ton."

"I had to bring my makeup case," she said in a hurt voice.

I added it to the pile. "Is that all?" I asked. "Are you sure you don't have a trunk somewhere in there?"

"I need clothes," Justine complained. "Who knows what the weather will be like tomorrow? Who knows what we'll decide to do? I like to come prepared, you know."

"It's going to be hot, Justine," Roni said dryly. "It's always hot in Phoenix in August. And I don't think we'll be going skiing."

I peeked into the car and saw Justine's stepmother smiling. She raised her eyebrows in mock despair. "Hi, Mrs. Craft," I said. "How's the baby?"

"She's doing well, thank you, Ginger."

"You didn't bring her," Roni complained, peering into the car.

"We left her sleeping at home. My husband's watching her," Mrs. Craft said. "You must come and see her. She's getting big and she smiles at everybody."

"The world's smartest baby," Justine commented. "Takes after me."

"Call me when you want to be picked up tomorrow, Justine," her stepmother said. "I'll bring the baby with me so you can all see her. Bye now. Don't stay up all night!"

"Yeah, right," Roni said, making us all laugh.

The car drove off and we headed for the house, dragging Justine's many items of luggage between us.

"How's the violin virtuoso?" Roni demanded, falling in step beside Karen.

"Don't say that," Karen said. "You should have seen how good all the other kids at the camp were.

I've had enough of violins! Especially because I associate violins with Jeremy."

"You wrote us about him," I said. "He was a pain, right?"

"Total pain, total nerd, totally embarrassing," Karen said. "Do you know he went out and picked wildflowers and put them on my breakfast tray—in front of the whole camp? And he composed a piece of music that he dedicated to me."

"Aw, how sweet," Roni teased.

"Don't knock it," Justine said. "Nobody ever composed a piece of music for me."

"Me neither," I said.

Karen made a face. "I wouldn't mind if Sting composed a piece for me, but a super-geek? The nerd to end all nerds? He wore a bow tie at camp! He polished his shoes every day. He quoted statistics at meals."

We were laughing as we made our way to my room. "Sounds like he'd be right at home with the nerd pack at our school," I said as I dumped Justine's sleeping bag on my bed.

"Don't mention them, please," Justine said. "I've had a great summer without a single nerd in sight. I'd almost forgotten they existed."

"You don't think a miracle happened and they've

decided to transfer to a magnet school for nerds, do you?" Roni quipped.

"Is there one?" Justine asked, wide-eyed.

Roni shoved her. "Get outa here," she said. "You'd believe anything, Justine."

"No, I wouldn't," she said, sounding offended. "I think it would be a great idea to have a magnet school for nerds. Then they could all be disgusting and nerdy together and not bother us!"

I looked from face to face. "It is so good to be back with you guys," I said. "Out there on the farm I thought I might never get back to normal life again."

Roni laughed. "Tell me about it! I'm convinced normal life doesn't exist in Mexico. I met only one cute boy the whole time I was there. My grandmother sent me to the market, and I saw this cute guy tinkering with a Mustang. So I went over to him and said, 'Hi, how do you like your American car? Is it giving you problems?' And he said, 'Maybe you can help me. The manual is in English.' So I translated for him and we got the car fixed and he gave me a soda from his ice chest and we chatted a while, then I went home. Well, you have no idea how fast rumor travels in small towns. By the time I got home, everyone knew that I'd been drinking Cokes with a strange guy. You'd have thought

I'd been dancing naked on the roof!"

She paused because we were all laughing. "It wasn't funny," she said. "My old aunts were all praying to saints and my grandmother was talking to her dead sister about me. After that they didn't let me out without an escort."

"I wish I'd had an escort." Karen sighed. "He could have kept Jeremy away from me."

Justine lay back on my bed against her rolled sleeping bag. "It seems like I'm the only one who had a killer summer," she said. "You should have seen the muscles on those lifeguards. Talk about hunks! I had to spend my whole summer fighting them off. Of course, there was a certain lifeguard called Larry. I didn't exactly fight him off." She closed her eyes with a satisfied smile.

"Tell us about him, Justine," Karen urged.

"High school senior at Del Mar. Water polo player—totally cute. We had the greatest time together. . . ."

"What did you do, Justine?" Roni asked. "Fake a drowning?"

"So what if I did?" Justine said. "Being carried up the beach in his strong arms was worth every second."

"Are you going to keep in touch with him?" I

asked. "Do you think you'll see him again?"

"Yeah, we'd love to meet him," Roni said.

"Are you crazy? Do you think I'd let you guys get within a mile of him?"

"We're your best friends, Justine," Karen said in a hurt voice. "You don't think we'd go after your guy?"

"Well, he is the cutest guy within five hundred miles," Justine said. "And you guys don't have boyfriends right now, except for Ginger, of course. She and Ben will still be dating when they're ninety-nine."

"They might be married by then, right, Ginger?" Karen commented.

I gave her what I hoped was a big smile. We'd only just gotten together again, so it wasn't the right time to bring up what was probably a stupid, groundless worry.

Roni collapsed into my armchair. "I'll tell you one thing," she said. "I am expecting great things to happen this year—new guy, new adventures. I'm not going to be boring old me anymore."

"You never were boring, Roni," Karen said. "You're one of the most un-boring people I know."

"Un-boring? Is that a real word?" I teased. "Don't forget we're in sophomore college-prep English this year."

"And you're a writer for the school newspaper, Karen. You should know about these things," Roni added.

Karen flushed and looked away with an embarrassed smile. "Cut it out, you guys," she said. "I haven't gotten back into the teasing mode yet."

"I'd forgotten that Karen is going to be on the newspaper staff," I said. "Now that you've moved up from cub reporter you'll have more assignments, right? Can you handle that with your violin practice?"

"I'll make time," Karen said firmly. "The newspaper is fun."

"Tell your folks it's a required activity," Justine said, making us all burst out laughing. That was what Karen had told her parents last year whenever she wanted to do something forbidden. Her folks are from Vietnam, and they're very, very strict. We had to come up with all kinds of little plots to make them let Karen do things that all normal teenagers do. They were a little more relaxed now, but they still watched over her like a hawk. And they were fanatical about her violin practice.

"I hope some cute guys are working on the paper this year," Karen said. "I need a new boyfriend too."

"Don't we all!" Justine blurted.

We looked at her in surprise. "What about the cute lifeguard, Justine?" I asked.

She turned bright red. "He was just a summer romance," she said. "Long-distance romances never work, do they? I have to be realistic."

"Aren't you at least going to write to each other?" Roni asked.

Justine shook her head. "It's better to break up when things are just perfect. That's what he told me when we said good-bye on the beach, in the moonlight."

Karen sighed. "How romantic. I wish someone would say something like that to me."

"Me too," I said. "Ben totally takes me for granted."

"Maybe you should think about a change too, Ginger," Justine said. "We could give the Boyfriend Club its first assignment for the new school year—to find four gorgeous guys within the first week."

We all laughed.

"That's some assignment," I said.

"The Boyfriend Club was never that good, Justine," Roni added.

"In fact, we never actually found a boyfriend for anybody, did we?" Karen agreed.

"At least not the ones we expected," I said.

"But we had fun anyway," Roni summed up. "And this year we'll do better. We've refined our skills. We know about life. We are more mature in our approach. You want four cute guys in the first week of school? No problem—let's go for it!"

Chapter

2

The next morning we woke to the sun streaming in through my window and to the smell of coffee coming from the kitchen. That had to mean it was pretty late. My dad never got up early on Sunday morning unless he was going fishing.

"What time is it?" Karen murmured from her sleeping bag on the floor.

"I don't know. My eyes won't open enough to focus on my alarm clock yet," I muttered.

"We must have stayed up half the night talking," Roni said, sitting up and stretching her arms. She gave a huge yawn.

"It *was* pretty late," I agreed.

"You'll never guess what I dreamed," Roni said,

climbing out of her sleeping bag.

"What?"

"I dreamed that we went shopping and there was this store at the mall called The Boyfriend Club. You could just look in a catalogue and say, 'I'd like that one, please,' and they brought the boy out to meet you."

"Hey, neat idea," I said, laughing. "I wonder if they would do boyfriend repairs, too?"

"Why?" Karen asked.

I could feel myself blushing. I hadn't meant to say that *Ben* needed repairing! I just shrugged at Karen.

Roni was watching me closely. "I think we should find a way to make Ben appreciate Ginger more," she said.

"Don't you dare," I replied. "I have enough problems with Ben without you butting in."

They both looked at me in surprise. "Problems?" cried Karen. "What problems? You never said you and Ben were having problems."

"Not really problems," I said quickly. "It's just that he's going to be a senior this year. Last year he was new at Alta Mesa too, and he didn't know anybody. But now he's on the football team and he knows everybody."

"So?"

"So I don't know whether he'll want to stick to the same girl," I finished.

"Good old adoring Ben?" Karen said. "Of course he will. You two were made for each other."

"I hope so," I said doubtfully.

Roni started to pick her way across the floor and stood looking down at Justine. "It's amazing how she can just sleep like that," she said. She tapped Justine's sleeping bag. "Time to wake up, sleepyhead."

"Go away," Justine muttered. "I'm finishing a nice dream."

We grinned at each other.

"Wake me when breakfast is ready," Justine continued, with her eyes still closed. "Pancakes stuffed with applesauce and topped with whipped cream and maple syrup, and maybe a side order of bacon."

"What do you think this is, the Hilton?" I demanded. "If you want pancakes, you get up and help cook them."

"Too tired," Justine whispered.

"I know how to get her up," Karen said with a laugh. She ran to the bathroom and came back with a glass of water. Then she dripped it onto Justine's face.

"What? Stop it! Cut it out!" Justine yowled, covering her head with her hands. Her eyes opened, and she glared up at Karen. "That's not fair! Now I'll have to style my hair again."

Karen just giggled.

Justine sat up and frowned. "If anyone ever thought you were a sweet, gentle person, Karen Nguyen, they were wrong."

"You'll survive, Justine," I said, laughing as I held out my hand to pull her up. "Come on, let's go get breakfast. I'm starving."

There was no sign of my dad in the kitchen. He often took his cup of coffee back to bed with the Sunday paper. "Great. We've got the kitchen to ourselves," I said. "My brother's not awake yet, if he's home. He might have spent the night over at Ben's. They were out late, I think."

"Out late? Where?"

"I don't know. Hanging with the guys, I guess."

"You let Ben go out late somewhere without you?" Justine demanded.

"He's got his own life, Justine, and he was Todd's best friend before he was my boyfriend."

"All the same," Justine said, "he shouldn't want to be out with other people. Maybe he *is* losing interest."

"I don't know what I can do about it," I said, feeling my heart drop into my stomach.

"Make him jealous," Roni suggested. "If he thought he might lose you, he'd wake up soon enough. Remember how worried he got when you had a crush on Scott Masters?"

"I know," I said, "but I couldn't go after another guy just to make Ben pay more attention to me. He's just busy, that's all. I'm sure everything will be fine. Now, who wants pancakes?"

The mention of food was enough to make us forget unimportant things like romance and school. I mixed while Roni sliced peaches, and Justine and Karen poured juice and set the table. I had just cooked the first stack of pancakes when the front door opened, sending in a blast of warm air that made the napkins fly off the counter. Todd came in, wearing old sweats, and stood gasping for breath. Ben followed him, holding onto the doorframe and panting.

"What's with you guys?" I asked.

"Ran all the way back from Ben's house," Todd gasped. "We did a hundred push-ups, a hundred sit-ups, pumped iron for an hour, and then ran flat out all the way here."

"Are you in training for Mr. Universe or just crazy?" Justine demanded.

"Football practice starts tomorrow," Ben ex-

34

plained. "We have to be in top shape."

"Yeah, don't forget that we're varsity now," Todd said, crossing the living room to the kitchen. "Ben's going to be the star wide receiver."

"Shut up, Todd," Ben said, giving him a shove. "Don't say stuff like that."

"It's true," Todd said. "You heard the coach. He said we're counting on you for the points this year, Campbell."

"Wooo, Ben," Roni said. "Way to go—college scholarship, big-time stuff, maybe turn pro?"

Ben looked very embarrassed. "I'm not that good. It's just that there isn't much talent at wide receiver this year. I'm all they've got."

"He's always too modest," Todd said.

I caught Ben's eye and got the message. "Stop talking about him in front of a bunch of girls, Todd," I said.

Todd laughed. "He better get used to being surrounded by girls this year. He's going to be Mr. Senior Hot-Shot Varsity Player. Adoring fans come with the territory." He leaned into the kitchen. "Great. You made us pancakes. I'm starving."

I snatched up the plate before he got it. "Get outa here. They're not for you. Cook your own if you want them."

"What's the point in having women around if they don't cook for you?" Todd teased. "You haven't been training her too well, Ben."

I waved a dripping spatula. "If you guys want to live to play football tomorrow, you better get away from this kitchen right now, or you'll find yourselves frying on that griddle."

"I think she means it, Todd." Ben laughed. "We better go shower."

"I don't know what you see in her," Todd said. The guys disappeared down the hall before I could hear Ben's answer. I shot my friends a despairing look. "Ugh, brothers," I snapped.

"They're lucky to have football," Roni commented. "It's not only a sport, it's like instant status. You're on the football team, you're somebody. Everyone in school knows you."

"Everyone knows you, Roni," I said. "You were one of the stars in the spring musical."

"And I better be one of the stars in the fall play too," Roni said.

"What play are they doing?"

"I haven't a clue. I'll have to wait until school starts to find out."

"And Karen will definitely be one of the stars in the school orchestra," I said thoughtfully. While I said it, I was wondering just what Ginger would be the star of this fall.

"And I've been thinking," Justine said, waving a piece of pancake on her fork. "Maybe I should try out for cheerleading again. They get to do all the fun stuff and they are definitely high-profile people."

Karen and I looked at each other in horror. "I don't think that's a great idea, Justine," Karen said quickly.

"You made the pyramid collapse at tryouts last year," I reminded her.

Justine made a face. "Okay, but that wasn't my fault. If those girls had been strong enough to support me . . ."

"You really want to be a cheerleader, Justine?" I asked. "Most of them are so snobby and phony. You always said that the girls at Sagebrush Academy were like that and you hated it."

Justine nodded. "Okay, so maybe I don't want to be a cheerleader. But I'd sure like to be a somebody this year."

"It will definitely be better than last year," I said. "We won't be little freshmen who don't know anybody."

The others went on talking about how wonderful sophomore year would be, smiling and laughing as they imagined all sorts of triumphs. There was a smile on my face too, but inside a scared feeling was growing. My friends all seemed to have something special to look forward to. I wasn't even sure I had a boyfriend anymore.

Of course, Ben hadn't come right out and said that he wanted to break up. But he *had* hinted at it. When we were together he seemed to like being with me, and he still looked at me in that special way. But he hadn't answered even one of my letters while I was in Texas, and when I came back, we'd had the weirdest conversation.

We had gone for a walk the evening I came back from Texas. It was a warm, dusty evening and the sun was sinking like a red fireball behind the mountains. Ben had looked pleased enough to see me, and he held my hand as we walked through the fields. But when we started talking about school, he cleared his throat, as if he was nervous.

"Ginger," he said slowly, "I feel like I should warn you in advance. I've got a lot of stuff to do this fall. I have really hard classes, and I've got to study for the SATs, and you know how much time football takes up. I'm going to be on varsity, remember."

He looked at me as if he was willing me to understand.

"So what are you trying to say?" I managed to ask.

He shrugged. "Nothing, really. Just that I want you to understand . . . if I don't have time for you, I mean."

I'd wanted to come right out and ask it: "Are you saying you want to break up before school starts?" But I couldn't do it. I was too scared of what the answer might be.

Chapter 3

"You know the best part of going back to school?" Justine asked as we got off the bus in the hot downtown sunshine. It was a Thursday afternoon—one of the last weekdays we'd be able to spend on our own for a whole school year!

"Being back in an atmosphere of learning? All those great books at your fingertips?" Roni suggested innocently.

"Get real." Justine gave her a friendly shove. "You know I've never opened a great book in my life and I don't intend to."

"Then how about the chance to meet new and exciting people and do new and exciting things?" Roni suggested.

"Cafeteria food?" I added.

"I'll tell you," Justine said, waving her arms dramatically in the direction of the mall's glittering steel and glass. "It's the back-to-school sales! New outfits, new shoes, new backpack. I just love that feeling of starting over with a new image each year, don't you?"

Roni and I exchanged glances. "I would if I had the money for a new image each year," I said.

"I, for one, don't intend to leave this mall today until I have a complete new designer outfit with co-ordinated accessories," Justine said.

I dug Roni in the side. "I might just have enough for a new designer scrunchie," I said. "How about you?"

Roni nodded. "I was thinking of designer shoe-laces," she said.

Justine gave me a worried look. "If it's a question of money, Ginger, I'm sure my father wouldn't notice a couple of extra outfits on the charge card. Or I could sacrifice and not go designer so we could get two outfits for the price of one."

Most of the time Justine annoyed me but sometimes she just blew me away with unexpected kindness. I tried to laugh it off. "I can't take your father's money, you dope," I said. "It was a sweet idea, but I'll put up with what I've got. I just hope there are

41

some good sales. These old Nikes are almost falling to pieces."

"You really should get more feminine shoes, Ginger," Justine said, looking down at my scuffed sneakers. "No wonder Ben is losing interest."

"I don't think he loves Ginger for her footwear," Roni commented.

"You know what I mean," Justine said. "She's going to have competition from all the cheerleaders this year. It's a big status thing to date a varsity player, especially one of the stars. Ginger's got to look sexy if she wants to compete."

"I can't change who I am," I said. "I've never been the feminine type. Ask Roni—she never saw me in a skirt until graduation from eighth grade."

Roni laughed. "And you never saw me *out* of a skirt until last year!"

"But skirts are really in now," Justine said. "I'm going to get one of those long crinkly gauze ones."

"I'd like one of them too," Roni said, "but I won't buy one, because I know my mother would smirk at me and say 'I told you so, Veronica.'"

We all laughed—except Karen. Suddenly I realized that she had hardly said a word since we'd met in the parking lot. She's often quieter than the rest of us, but today she was *way* too quiet.

"Are you okay, Karen?" I asked. "You've been aw-fully quiet, even for you."

"Yeah, Karen," Roni chimed in. "You haven't said a word. Are you sick?"

Karen managed a weak smile. "It's nothing," she said. "Just a personal problem."

"If it's anything we can help with, you know you've just got to ask," I said.

She shook her head, and I was surprised to see that she was squeezing back tears. "Nobody can help, thanks. It's something I have to sort out for myself."

Justine put an arm around her shoulders. "I know, let's go straight to the ice cream parlor and have a giant Matterhorn sundae—my treat. That will cheer you up. It always works for me."

Karen's eyes were still full of tears. "I'm afraid it's more than a one-Matterhorn problem, Justine," she said. "I thought I had it all under control until I was with you guys. Now I realize how hard it really is."

"You mean *we're* your problem?" I asked, stunned.

"I really don't want to talk about it anymore," Karen said, turning her head away. "I'm just not ready yet."

"Okay. Let's go shopping," Justine said. She pushed open the mall door and we were met by a welcome breeze of air conditioning. "I always go shopping to make me forget my problems. Maybe it will work for Karen too."

I studied Karen's back as she walked ahead of us. Obviously she'd had some sort of fight with her parents again. It wasn't easy having parents who had grown up in a totally different culture, I could see that. She'd had to fight hard last year to do the things we all took for granted, like go to the freshman welcome dance or even sleep over at my house.

"Okay, which store first?" Justine asked, looking up and down the palm-lined hallways. "Macy's is at one end. They might have nice things, but the Something Special boutique is the other way."

"Nobody else can afford anything from Something Special, Justine," Roni said. "Let's head toward Macy's and look at some of the other clothes on the way. The music store's that way too. Maybe I'll go without clothes and buy myself a new CD. Who needs new clothes?"

"Go without clothes?" Justine looked horrified. "How could you possibly think that way, Roni?"

Roni grinned at me and Karen. She loves to tease Justine.

We were halfway down the mall when a strange laugh rang out, echoing from the marble and glass over the tasteful piped background music. It sounded like a cross between a hyena in pain and a whooping crane doing its whoops. (Actually I've never heard a whooping crane, but it's how I imagine they'd sound.) Only one person in the world had a laugh like that. We froze.

"It's Owen," Roni whispered.

"That has to mean the nerds are here," Justine exclaimed, wrinkling her nose in disgust. "What should we do?"

We glanced around for an escape route, but we were halfway between exits.

"Keep going," I said. "Head for the nearest clothing store." However rude we tried to be to Alta Mesa High's nerd pack, they never got the hint that we found them repulsive. "If we bump into the nerds we say 'Hi, we're in a hurry,' and we keep on going. They'd never follow us into a women's clothing store."

"Want to bet?" Justine demanded. "They don't get embarrassed by the things that would make normal humans die of humiliation. They'd follow us into the fitting rooms."

"Ewww," Roni said.

"I bet the nerds will seem normal after Jeremy," Karen muttered.

"Are you serious?" Justine asked. "He can't have been that bad."

"Believe it," Karen said. "The happiest day of my life was when we drove to the airport from music camp."

"Poor Karen. You've had your share of problems recently, haven't you?" Roni said sympathetically. Hastily she added, "Sorry, I promised we wouldn't talk about it. Forget I said that."

"I wonder where the nerds are lurking?" Justine asked. "I don't hear Owen. Do you think they've got a secret entrance to the mall from their underground slime cave?"

"What a horrible thought, Justine," I said. "Imagine innocently walking through the mall, when suddenly the floor opens up and a squeaky little voice says—"

"Well, hello there, girls. This is indeed a pleasant surprise!"

The voice sounded close enough to touch! We spun around, nearly knocking over a potted palm tree, and there they were, grinning their hideous grins at us. We just stood with our mouths open. Our fight-or-flight mechanism must have been put out of action by what we saw. The voice had been Owen's. The laugh had been Owen's. But the person before us now, grinning Owen's leering grin, didn't look like Owen at all. He was taller than us and dressed in a button-down dress shirt, a striped tie, and dark pants. Behind him stood the rest of the nerd pack in various shapes and sizes.

"Owen, is that you?" Roni stammered.

"Owen, you're not a shrimp anymore," Justine said in her usual tactless way. "What happened? Did your creepy friends invent a growing powder?"

Owen looked offended. "It's called puberty, if you must know," he said. "About the age of fourteen or fifteen, it is natural for young men to encounter a growth spurt."

"Owen is now close to manhood," Ronald agreed, blinking at us excitedly. "The time is coming to choose his mate. How about it? Which of you would like to be the lucky lady to be Owen's first date?"

"Thank you, but we don't date outside our species," Justine said coldly.

I pressed my lips together and didn't look at Roni, because she would make me laugh for sure. I felt sorry for the nerds. Lots of kids at school gave them a hard time, so I didn't want to hurt their feelings any more. The trouble was, they took anything other than outright rudeness as encouragement, and I certainly didn't want that!

47

"Don't worry, Owen. Ms. Right is waiting for you out there somewhere," Ronald said, putting his hand on Owen's shoulder.

"On a very distant planet," Justine muttered into my ear.

I tried hard not to laugh. "We have to get going, guys. We're in a big hurry," I said.

"Yeah, the stores might run out of sale items," Roni added.

Owen's face lit up. "You're here for the back-to-school sale? So are we."

Justine looked astonished. "You guys are clothes shopping?"

"Clothes?" Owen squeaked. Actually his voice now hovered between a squeak and a growl. "Who said anything about clothes?"

"We're going to the office-supply store," Ronald said.

Immediately Roni grabbed my arm. "We've got to go," she called over her shoulder. "Have fun shopping for . . . supplies."

"See you in school, ladies," Owen called after us loudly enough to make half the mall look in our direction.

"Not if we see you first," Justine murmured.

"That convinces me," Roni said. "The Boyfriend

Club has got to work overtime. We need new boyfriends before the welcome dance or we don't go. There is no way I'm going to be trapped by nerds like last year."

"I agree," Justine said. "Somehow we have to come up with cute guys during the first week of school."

"I know." Roni looked at Karen. "You can run an ad in the school newspaper! You could do that for us, couldn't you, Karen?"

Usually Karen would have come back with a witty reply to a question like this. She's very quick. But she just shook her head without saying a word.

"Come on, Karen. Cheer up," I said. "I'm sure it's not as bad as you think."

"It's worse," Karen whispered. She gulped as if she was swallowing back a sob. "I won't be able to run the ad in the newspaper. I won't even be able to go to the welcome dance! I won't be coming back to school with you guys."

"You what?" I stammered.

"I'm not coming back to Alta Mesa."

"Why not?"

She sighed. "It's kind of complicated," she said.

Roni took her arm. "Let's go sit on that bench and you can tell us."

49

We fought our way across the stream of people to a bench by a window.

"Do your parents still think we're a bad influence on you?" Justine asked. "They're not sending you back to Catholic school, are they?"

She shook her head. "Worse than that," she said. "I won a scholarship to the Arizona Conservatory of Music."

"But Karen, that's wonderful. Congratulations."

"That's what my parents think," Karen said. "They're so proud, they're going around telling half the state. That's why I didn't have the heart to turn it down. But it means I can't go to Alta Mesa. The course at the conservatory is full time. They send us to the high school across the street for the math classes and stuff that they don't offer. But it means that I'll be a full-time music student from now on."

"Is that what you really want, Karen?" Roni asked quietly. "I got the feeling that you weren't sure if music was really for you."

Karen sighed again. "I don't know. Part of me is really flattered and excited. They only take the very best. My teacher says that giving me a scholarship means that they think I have a great future."

"Wow, Karen," Justine said. "And to think we

knew you way back when. Do we get tickets to your opening at Carnegie Hall?"

"That's the problem," Karen said. "I'm not sure I *want* a great future. I wouldn't mind playing in an orchestra, but when I think of being a soloist, I get the worst butterflies inside."

"I'm sure that would get better when you're used to it," I said.

"You all sound like you're glad I'm going," Karen mumbled.

"We didn't mean it that way," Roni said quickly. "Of course we're not glad to be losing you, but we're really excited for you. You're getting a chance most people only dream of. If someone offered me a scholarship to an acting academy, I'd take it."

"I don't think they have academies for hams," I said. I was trying to lighten things up, but nobody laughed.

How could we possibly go back to school without Karen?

Chapter 4

"It's funny," Roni said on the bus home. "Just when you think you've got your whole route through life planned out, they change the signs and the road goes off in a different direction."

"Very deep," I said. "You're turning into a regular philosopher."

"I think I read it somewhere," Roni confessed. "On the back of a matchbook, maybe. But it's true. We were so sure we were going to have a killer sophomore year."

"We still can," I said. "We can do all the things we planned. It's just that Karen won't be there to share them with us."

Roni sighed. "Karen's always the one who makes

the rest of us feel better when we're upset. Why couldn't Justine have gone instead?"

"Oh, come on," I said. "We would miss Justine as much as Karen."

"You're right. Justine was upset too. She didn't even buy anything today."

"We can still get together on weekends. Karen can still come to our sleepovers," I said, trying to cheer myself up as much as Roni.

"Sure," she said.

We got off at our stop and walked home together. Even before we got close to Roni's house, we could hear her little brother's high-pitched voice as he played in their front yard.

"I feel like my whole world's changing," Roni said. "Paco's going to start kindergarten. It seems like only yesterday he was a little baby."

"Grandma Roni remembers," I said, laughing at her tragic face. "Cheer up. You've still got me."

"That's what's depressing me," she quipped. "Who'd want to be stuck with you?"

"Thanks a lot. I know when I'm not wanted," I said, pretending to be hurt. I stalked off down the street, smiling to myself. As long as Roni was around, everything would be okay.

❖　　❖　　❖

"Ginger? It's Justine." Her voice was light and nervous. I had been annoyed when the phone rang. After all, I'd been busy thinking about school and how miserable it would be without Karen. The last thing I wanted was to be interrupted.

"What's up?"

"Plenty," said Justine. "My dad called from England last night."

"I thought he called every night."

"He does. Shut up and listen. This is important. He said it looks like his business there is going to drag on and on. They've taken over a company, you know, and he has to get it on its feet. . . ."

"So?"

"So he doesn't want to be away from Alexandra and Christine. He feels like he's missing all those important milestones in the baby's life—you know, her first smile, the day she turned over. Parents are really into that stuff."

"So he's coming home?"

"No, the opposite. He wants us to go over there!"

"To England? Are you serious? For how long?"

"Until he gets the job done. About a year, maybe," she said.

"A year! What about school?"

"He said he'd look into schools over there for me."

"Wow," I said. "I don't know what to say. Are you happy about this?"

"I guess so," Justine said. "I've always loved London, and it will be a big opportunity for me. Who knows? I might even meet an English lord. Can't you just see me as Lady Justine? You'd have to curtsy, of course."

"Of course," I said automatically. I was still in shock. First Karen and now this. "There won't be much of a Boyfriend Club left, without you and Karen," I said.

"I know," Justine answered. "That's the only reason I don't want to go. I hate the thought of being away from you guys for a year. But I guess I don't have much choice. Christine's already talking to real estate people about leasing the house while we're gone. I can't live here alone."

"We'll miss you, Justine," I said. I really meant it. It wouldn't be the same without her.

"Will you tell Roni for me?" she asked. Her voice was shaky. "I'm going to cry if I have to go through this two more times."

"Sure. I'll go over there right now," I said. "She's baby-sitting her little brother."

"I've got so much to do," Justine said loudly, as if she was trying to *make* herself be happy about moving. "Do you realize that none of my wardrobe is suitable for London? I need the tailored look, dark colors, wool jackets . . . so much shopping, so little time. Gotta go, Ginger."

I stood staring at the phone long after she hung up. Then I headed down the street to Roni's house.

"You won't believe this," I said as I let myself in. "Justine's moving to England." And I told her all the details.

"Some people have all the luck," Roni complained. "What I wouldn't give for a year in Europe. She'll be insufferable when she comes back! She'll tell us what she said to the queen when they had tea together . . ."

"And how terribly, frightfully primitive we are out here in the colonies," I finished for her.

We smiled, but it was a sad smile.

"Looks like it's just you and me, kid," Roni said. "Just like when we started."

I nodded. "At least we're not freshmen this year. We know people now. We'll do just fine."

"Sure we will. Only it won't be the same."

"No," I said. "It won't be the same."

Paco came into the room and proudly showed us how he could write his name.

"Where's your mom today?" I asked.

Roni shrugged. "I don't know. She just said she had to go out. I hope she's buying us ice cream, right, Paco?"

"You want to do something this afternoon after your mother gets back?" I asked.

"Like what?"

"Go somewhere to cheer us up? A movie, maybe?"

"I don't know if I can afford a movie. I still need clothes for school."

"Then we'll go clothes shopping together, just the two of us. That way we don't have to be embarrassed if we go to the discount stores. I'll never tell if you don't."

Roni laughed. "It's a deal," she said.

I was just getting ready to leave when Roni's mom burst in through the front door. Her face was flushed and excited. We all looked up as she put down her purse and smoothed back her flyaway hair.

"Is something wrong, Mama?" Roni asked.

"Wrong? Why?"

"You look upset."

"Not upset. Just shaken up," she said. "I still can't believe I did it."

"Did what, Mama?"

"Got a job," Mrs. Ruiz said. "I went out and got myself a job."

"A job?" Roni asked suspiciously. "What kind of job?"

"Nothing fancy," Mrs. Ruiz said in her halting English. "Just in a bakery at the mall. But it's a start. I never worked in America before. I have to start somewhere."

"Good for you, Mrs. Ruiz," I said. "It's not easy to get a job when you haven't worked for so many years."

"You're right," she said. "It's not easy. I never believed they'd hire me, but they did. I'm so pleased. I was worried about saving money for Roni's college, and then the little ones too. They're smart. They'll need a college education if they want to make something of their lives. But it costs so much money. Now I'll be able to save a little."

Roni threw her arms around her mother. "You're the best," she said. "I'm really proud of you, Mama. And I'm going to make you really proud of me too."

Mrs. Ruiz smiled and wiped away a tear.

"I'm proud too, Mama," Paco said, running over to hug her legs.

"What's going to happen to him?" Roni asked, indicating her little brother. "Will he have to go to day care?"

"He starts kindergarten, remember?" Mrs. Ruiz

said. "I have to work from noon until five. I can sign him up for the afternoon session. That doesn't get out until three. You can pick him up and look after him and the girls until I get home."

"Wait a minute," Roni said. "That won't work, Mama. I don't get back here until four, even on good days. When I have stuff after school, I'm not home until five or later."

"I know that," Mrs. Ruiz said. "But I did some thinking. I'm sure they would let you transfer back to Oak Creek High School if we told them of our problem. They get out at two thirty, and you'd be close enough to pick up your brother."

"Oak Creek High?" Roni shrieked. "You can't be serious. I like it at Alta Mesa, Mama. I don't want to transfer."

"And I don't really want to work in a bakery, but I'll do it," Mrs. Ruiz said. "It's for you, Roni. For your future I do this."

"I won't have a future if I go to Oak Creek," Roni argued. "It's a school for farm kids, Mama. They don't have any good classes and the kids are all hicks!"

"I'm sure they have some good teachers there," Mrs. Ruiz said. "Mrs. Paez's son Emilio got a scholarship to the university from that school."

"Because he plays football, Mama. That's all they care about there. No drama, no music, nothing. Just bonehead classes and football."

Mrs. Ruiz held up her hand. "We won't talk about it until your father gets home. Then you come with us to meet the principal. I'm sure he will tell you that there are good classes for a girl who wishes to go to college. I'm sure they will be happy to have you there."

"I can't believe this," Roni said. "You're going to work so that I can go to college, but if I go to Oak Creek, I probably won't even get into college. It doesn't make sense."

"Like I said, Veronica, we'll discuss it when your father gets home. Until then, no more."

Roni gave me a despairing look.

"I guess I should be going," I said.

"I'll walk home with you," Roni offered.

I shook my head. "You better stay here," I said.

"Ginger," Roni said, "what are we going to do?"

"Don't ask me," I said. "It looks like I'm the only person still going to Alta Mesa."

I started for the door.

"You could come to Oak Creek too," Roni called after me. "We'd have fun there together. . . ."

"I don't want to go to Oak Creek," I said. "I like it

60

where I am. Why does everything have to change?"

I stepped out into the hot sun and started running. I ran all the way back to my house, even though I could feel the sweat trickling down my face. At least, I told myself it was sweat. I didn't want to admit it was tears.

"Hey!" A large shape stepped out in front of me and big hands grabbed my shoulders. "I thought I was the one in serious training. What's the big hurry?"

I looked up into Ben's smiling face. The smile faded as he noticed the tears. "Ginger, what's wrong?"

"Everything," I said. "First Karen and then Justine and now Roni—"

"You had a fight with them?"

"No." I shook my head, trying to compose myself enough to get the words out. "They're all leaving, Ben. They won't be coming back to school. Karen's going to music school and Justine's going to England and now Roni's got to transfer to Oak Creek." I tried to swallow back my sob, but it came out like a giant hiccup. "I'll be all alone at Alta Mesa. I'll have nobody."

His strong arms came around me. "Yes, you will," he said softly. "You'll still have me."

He pulled me close and held me tightly. I rested my head against his chest, closing my eyes and just absorbing his warmth and closeness. A great feeling of peace came over me. If Ben still loved me, I could handle anything, even losing my three best friends. At that moment I really believed that everything just might be okay after all.

Chapter 5

I even sang as I fixed dinner that night. Ben still cared about me. I could handle anything now that I knew that. I could walk across deserts or climb mountains if Ben was waiting for me on the other side. I told myself that I'd overreacted and that everything was going to be okay. Roni wouldn't really have to go to dumb old Oak Creek, not when she got a chance to talk to her dad about it. He'd take her side and say that she should stay at Alta Mesa. It would be the way it was before—just the two of us. Maybe we'd try out for a team together, or maybe I'd go back to the ecology club and Roni would star in the play. As long as Ben still cared, it all seemed possible.

I stayed in an upbeat mood until my father arrived home that evening.

"Good news, kids," he yelled as he slammed the front door behind him.

"We won the lottery?" Todd asked, looking up from the TV.

"Not that good."

"You're getting Ginger married off into a harem in Saudi Arabia?"

"Shut up, Todd. Let Dad talk," I said. "What is it, Dad?"

"I've found a place for Uncle Elmer," he said.

"You what?" Todd and I looked at each other, puzzled. "What kind of place?"

"I convinced him that he couldn't go on working the farm after the heart surgery," Dad said, "so he asked me to keep my eyes open around here. Well, I've done it. I found him a job with a farm machinery dealership, and I even found a nice little house for them to rent until they decide whether they want to make it permanent out here."

"Let me get this straight," I said. "Uncle Elmer and Aunt Lorraine are moving here? To Phoenix?"

"That's what I said. Right here to Oak Creek. I found them a place on Cottonwood."

"On Cottonwood?" That was only two streets

away. "And they're all moving here? All of them—including Lacey?"

Dad rolled his eyes. "What do you think? They'd leave their daughter alone on the farm? Of course they're all coming, in time for school to start."

A feeling of doom came over me. I could see Lacey in her overalls, looking like something out of the cast of *Oklahoma!*, following me everywhere I went. "S-she's not going to Alta Mesa, is she?" I stammered.

"Why not? I told Uncle Elmer it's a good school."

"She'd be more at home at Oak Creek," I said quickly. "All the farm kids go there."

"That's precisely why she should go to Alta Mesa," Dad snapped. I could tell he was losing his patience with me. "Uncle Elmer wants the best for his kids. That's one of the reasons they decided to give up the farm. I told them you'd take good care of Lacey and show her the ropes."

I must have visibly shuddered.

"There's nothing wrong with Lacey," Dad said sternly.

"Are you kidding? Dad, she drives me crazy! She never left me alone when I was there. When she wasn't asking dumb questions, she was telling me how I was doing everything wrong!"

"I thought she was a nice kid," Dad said. "A little countrified, maybe, but she'll soon learn to fit in if you help her—which I expect you to do, Ginger. Lacey is your cousin, whether you like her or not. Family helps family. Don't forget that. Those kids aren't monsters."

"You didn't have to live there with them for a month, Dad," Todd said. For once I agreed with him. "You were only there a week. And you didn't have to share a room with the boys. I don't know about Lacey, but Bif and Bart put a frog in my bed."

"What's so bad about that? That's just high spirits," Dad said. "Good-natured fun."

"Huh," I snapped.

"This is my brother we're talking about here," Dad said. "I want to make sure everything goes smoothly for him, understand?"

"Yes, Dad," Todd and I grumbled.

I rushed to my room and called Roni.

"I'm glad you called," she said before I could say anything. "I was about to call you."

"Did your dad take your side about Oak Creek?"

"No way. He thinks it's a great idea for me to go back there. He said he never liked the thought of me going to school so far away from home, and now I can hang out with the neighborhood kids again."

"Has he taken a good look at the neighborhood kids?" I demanded. "Think back to middle school, Roni—Joe Garcia and Al Peters and all those gross boys!"

"Don't remind me," Roni said with a sigh. "How am I ever going to survive, Ginger? Can't you think of a way to make my parents change their minds?"

"I wish I could," I said.

"Do you think your dad would adopt me?" she said, half laughing. "You always said you wanted a sister."

"I'd rather have you than the family I'm about to be stuck with," I said.

"What family?"

"I didn't think I could possibly get any more bad news in one day, but I was wrong. My cousin Lacey is moving here."

"The one from the boonies?"

"That's the one. And there's more. She's going to Alta Mesa with me."

"At least you won't be all alone," Roni said.

"Are you kidding? I'd rather be all alone. I'd rather be anywhere in the world than with my cousin Lacey. You can't imagine how annoying she is, Roni. She has this horrible donkey laugh and she stands right up close to you and breathes down your neck and nudges you every time she thinks something's funny."

"Sounds pretty terrible," Roni agreed. "You'll just have to whip her into shape before school starts."

"If I was smart, I'd take her up to the top of Spirit Rock and lose her there," I said. "Why did everything have to go wrong like this, Roni? It's not fair!"

"You shouldn't complain," she said. "At least you still get to go to Alta Mesa. Think of me at Oak Creek with all the pickup trucks and cowboy boots! Your cousin Lacey would be totally at home there!"

"There has to be a way to make your parents see sense, Roni," I said. "Let's get together with Karen and Justine. Four heads are better than one. Maybe they'll come up with a great idea."

"Yeah, like smuggling me to England in Justine's suitcase," Roni said grimly. "This whole thing seems like a bad dream."

"Hang in there," I said. "At least you won't have an embarrassing cousin following you around."

"Maybe Lacey will be so blown away by the big city that she'll be too shy to say a word," Roni suggested. "And she'll be impressed when she sees how popular you are at school."

"Popular, me?"

"You are," Roni said. "You get along with every-one. You did great in track."

"Not as great as you did in the play."

Roni sighed. "I bet they don't even have drama at Oak Creek. I bet they don't have anything for girls except cheerleading." She looked at me sadly. "It will be the first time we've been apart, Ginger," she said. "What am I going to do without you?"

      ❖   ❖   ❖

We didn't have time for a Boyfriend Club sleep-over before Lacey's family rolled into town. Unfortunately I was the only one home when they arrived. Their old truck was piled high and they looked exactly like the opening scene from *The Beverly Hillbillies*. I just prayed that nobody I knew was around.

Lacey came bounding toward me like a large Saint Bernard puppy, her ginger braids flying out behind her. My hair is sort of strawberry blond, but hers is real carrot. And her face is totally covered in freckles.

"Cousin Ginger," she yelled, nearly crushing my ribs as she hugged me. "I can't tell you how excited I am to be living in the big city and going to a real fine city school!"

I led her down the front path and into the house. "You know, Lacey, it will take some getting used to. Even I found it hard when I started. It's so huge I kept getting lost and winding up in the wrong classes. I even thought of tying a string to my locker."

"Aw, go on with you," she said, giving me a friendly shove that nearly sent me sprawling into the flower beds.

"I'm serious," I said. "It was scary being surrounded by three thousand strangers. The halls are so full, the kids just push you out of the way if you don't move in time."

"Mercy," Lacey said. "You don't say, Cousin Ginger?"

"Yep," I said. "At least you've got muscles from lifting all those bales of hay. Maybe they won't push you so easily."

She nodded. "And I hope you've brought something other than overalls," I continued. "Alta Mesa is a city school. The kids there are really fashion-conscious. My friend Justine never wears the same outfit twice in a semester."

"Mercy," Lacey said again.

"And of course there are a lot of snobby girls—all

the cheerleaders, for example—who just love to make fun of you if you don't look right." I put a hand on her arm. "But don't worry. We have time before school starts to go shopping and get you a complete new look."

"A complete new look?" she stammered. "I don't have that kind of money, Ginger. You know that."

"Then maybe my friends can help give you a makeover," I said. "You know, give you some makeup tips and restyle your hair."

"Makeup? Shoot, I don't wear makeup."

"My point precisely," I said with a superior smile. I didn't usually wear makeup myself, but I was enjoying this. For four weeks I'd had to put up with Lacey's annoying donkey laugh every time I did something dumb around the farm. Now it was my turn.

"You have a lot to learn in a little time, Lacey," I said. "The way you look, the way you speak, the way you touch people—it's all got to go. Kids don't behave like that around here. You'll be laughed at."

"Gee, Ginger, I never thought of that before," Lacey said. "I'd sure appreciate it if you helped me."

I went into the kitchen and got out a jug of cold lemonade. My two bratty boy cousins had already disappeared somewhere, probably tearing apart the neighborhood. My uncle and aunt sat gratefully under the ceiling fan.

"Was that drive ever hot. Woo-ee," Aunt Lorraine said. "I sure appreciate this, Ginger," she added as I poured the lemonade.

"It's real nice to see how Lacey and Ginger get along so well," I heard Uncle Elmer remark to Aunt Lorraine. "And you were worrying that she wouldn't fit in here."

I smiled sweetly. "I've just been telling Lacey about my school."

"She's looking forward to that, aren't you, Lacey?" Aunt Lorraine asked. "She talked about nothing else all the way here."

"There's a truck pulling into your driveway, Cousin Ginger," Lacey yelled, running over to the window.

"Oh, that must be Todd home from football practice," I said.

"Who's that other guy?" Lacey asked.

"That's Ben," I said. "He's . . . Todd's best friend."

"What a hunk," Lacey said. "Look at those muscles."

I was trying to think of a polite way to tell her that Ben was not up for grabs when the boys came rushing in. "Dying," Todd gasped. "Cold

72

drink." He looked surprised at the strange faces. "Oh, hi, Uncle Elmer. Hi, Aunt Lorraine. Welcome to Phoenix." He poured himself a huge glass of lemonade and drained it in one gulp. I poured one for Ben and handed it to him.

"Thanks," he gasped. "Do you know how hot it is out there? And the coach made us practice sprint drills!"

"Ben," I said. "This is my aunt and uncle from Texas who are moving here."

"And this is our daughter, Lacey," Uncle Elmer said. "Go on, Lacey, say howdy to the young man."

Lacey stuck out her hand awkwardly. "Howdy," she said. "I'm Lacey. I'm real pleased to meet ya." She pumped Ben's hand as if she was trying to shake his arm out of his socket.

Ben shot me an amused look.

"We have to go," Todd said. "We just stopped off for a drink, but we're meeting some other guys over at Ben's. See you later."

As soon as the door closed, Uncle Elmer nudged Lacey. She was still gazing at the door. "See, Lacey, what did I tell you? And you were scared that all the boys here would be wimpy and citified. There's a young man with a fine set of muscles right on your doorstep."

She had gone over to the window to watch Ben's truck drive away, so I couldn't make eye contact with her.

"He sure is fine," she said.

Just wait until I get you alone, Lacey Hartman, I thought. *I might have to show you around and make you welcome, but Ben is mine.*

Chapter

6

"Take Lacey along with you and introduce her to your friends," my father said when I told him I wanted to sleep over at Justine's house on Friday night.

"Oh, come on, Dad." I sighed. "She doesn't need to meet my friends. None of them is going to Alta Mesa this year anyway, so what's the point?"

"The point is that she's all alone and she needs to feel like she belongs here," he said.

"Dad, I really don't want—" I began.

"She's going with you and that's final, Ginger," he said. "Or you don't go either." Usually it was pretty easy to get around my dad, but for some reason anything to do with Uncle Elmer and his family brought out his stubbornness.

I gave another dramatic sigh as I went to my room to call Justine with the terrible news. At least it would be fun to watch Lacey's face as we opened the wrought-iron gates at the impressive driveway to Justine's mansion.

"Do you want to come with me to sleep over at my friend's house?" I asked Lacey when she came around that afternoon.

"Are you sure I'm welcome?" she asked. "I wouldn't want to be in the way."

"It's nothing special," I said. "Just my best friends and I hanging out together. It will give you a chance to get to know people and see how we have fun in the big city."

"I'd sure like that, Cousin Ginger," she said. "I appreciate the offer."

"Lacey, you sound like something out of *Little House on the Prairie*. Stop calling me Cousin Ginger."

"Sorry, Cous—I mean, Ginger."

"Oh, and bring a bathing suit," I said. "We usually go swimming."

"Is there a pool nearby? That would be wonderful," she said.

Just you wait until you see how wonderful, I

thought as we took the bus to Justine's house. Lacey would be so impressed when she saw what kind of friends I had! Then it hit me. I wouldn't have these friends anymore. This was probably the last time I'd be hanging out at Justine's. In all the upheaval of Lacey's arrival, I'd forgotten that I'd be losing my best friends.

We got off the bus and started walking along Justine's street.

"What a fancy neighborhood," Lacey exclaimed. "Look at all these big cars! That house has a swimming pool. Are you sure this isn't Hollywood?"

"No, just plain old Phoenix," I said smoothly.

I pushed open Justine's gate.

"Holy cow!" Lacey exclaimed. "This is a real, live, honest-to-goodness mansion. Your friend lives here?"

"Believe it, Lacey," I said.

I was enjoying every moment until the front door opened.

"Ginger," Justine exclaimed as if she hadn't seen me for ages. Her eyes were very bright and she looked as if she might have been crying. "I can't believe this is the last time we'll be doing this. The others are already here. Come on in."

"This is my cousin Lacey," I said. "Lacey, this is Justine."

"Hi, Lacey," Justine said. "Sorry the place is a mess right now. We're moving to England."

For once, Lacey was speechless. She followed Justine and me into the marble entry hall, where some big boxes were already stacked.

"I've been packing up my room," Justine said. "It's so hard, Ginger. And I don't mean deciding what to take with me. It just hit me that I won't be seeing you guys again."

I headed for the stairs, but Justine stopped me. "The others are out back," she said. "We were waiting for you to go swimming."

She led us to the back patio, where Karen and Roni were lying on loungers under the palm trees by the pool.

"Holy cow," Lacey said again. "Is your dad a movie star or something?"

"No, why?" Justine asked.

"The big house and the swimming pool and everything."

"Everyone around here has a pool," Justine said. "You need it in this heat."

"It gets pretty hot back home in Texas," Lacey said, "but we just go down to the old swimming hole, right, Cousin Ginger?"

"And it's full of crawdads or whatever those

creepy things were," I added with a shudder. "Something nipped me on the leg, and I never went in there again."

"It's about time you two got here," Karen called. "We've been waiting for you."

"There's ice cream in the freezer in the cabana," Roni added. "We left some for you."

I introduced Lacey.

"So you're Roni," she said. "I've heard a lot about you."

"Only good things, I hope."

"I heard how you two have been best friends since you were little bitty girls," Lacey said, "and how you always do everything together."

"Not anymore," Roni said. "My folks are sending me to another school—"

"Let's go change, Lacey," I said. I didn't want to talk about the fact that I was going to be alone at Alta Mesa with Lacey. I didn't even want to think about it.

As soon as Lacey had changed into her brightly flowered bathing suit, she did a cannonball into the pool. "Come on, Cousin Ginger. This is real fun," she yelled. "Don't be a scaredy cat." She splashed across the pool at me. "Come slide with me. Yahoo!"

"If she's going to Alta Mesa," Roni muttered in my ear, "someone better clue her in very quickly,

79

or you'll die of embarrassment."

"No kidding," I mouthed back as I was dragged underwater by Lacey's strong hand.

After our swim, we lay out in the shade, drying off. Lacey wandered around taking in the wonders of Justine's backyard, yelling from time to time when she discovered the hot tub or the fountain spilling over rocks.

"I can't believe that in a couple of weeks I'll be freezing my buns off in London," Justine said. "I'm going to have to shop like crazy when I get there. I have no warm clothes."

"I wonder if you'll have to wear a uniform," Karen said.

"A uniform? Are you out of your mind?"

"Most English schools require it."

"I'd rather die. There has to be an American school in London, doesn't there?"

"Don't worry, Justine," I cut in. "You'll get to do stuff the rest of us only dream of. You can just pop through that Channel tunnel to Paris. Remember how we all talked about going there?"

"Paris." Roni sighed. "What I wouldn't give to go to Paris."

"Paris?" Lacey cut in. "I went there once. Wasn't much of a place at all."

"Paris? You went to Paris?" I couldn't have been more surprised. "When did you ever go to Paris?"

"The time we went to Houston," Lacey said. "We had a cousin over in Beaumont and we stopped off in Paris on the way."

I started to giggle. "Lacey, we're not talking about Paris, Texas," I said. "We're talking about Paris, France."

"Oh," she said, turning bright red. "How was I supposed to know that?"

Justine shrieked with laughter. "Paris, Texas. I love it!"

Roni and Karen were laughing too.

Lacey's face turned even redder.

"Cut it out, you guys," she said. "I feel like a jerk."

"It's okay, Lacey," Karen said kindly. "How were you to know?"

Justine shook her head. "Just don't go around saying stuff like that too loudly at Alta Mesa, okay?"

Lacey looked down at her feet. "I don't even want to go to dumb ole Alta Mesa," she said. "I won't know what to say there. I won't know how to act. I've never been in a house with a swimming pool before, or to Paris, France. Kids will laugh at me. I'll be a freak."

"No, you won't, Lacey," I said.

"Sure I will. Y'all laughed when I got that Paris thing wrong."

"That was funny," I agreed.

"See? I'll be saying the wrong thing and doing the wrong thing all the time and y'all will be having a good laugh at my expense."

"Don't worry, Lacey," Roni said. "We'll help you know how to act. Won't we, Ginger?" She stared straight at me.

"Oh, uh, sure we will," I agreed hastily.

"I know. We'll give you a makeover," Justine said excitedly. "I love doing makeovers, and you need one in the worst way, if you don't mind my saying so."

"Justine!" Karen hissed, nudging her.

"Well, it's true," Justine said. "I'm sorry, but she looks like something straight from the pioneer days."

"I know I do," Lacey said. "But I don't know how I can change the way I look. I don't have the money to go to fancy stores or fancy beauty parlors."

"You have us, right here," Justine said, scrambling to her feet. "You are talking to the most coordinated, best-dressed person at Alta Mesa High. Not only do I have the best wardrobe, I also have a certain flair for these things, a certain inborn grace and style . . . Aahhhhhh!"

She had been stepping away from us, waving her

arms grandly as she talked. I could see that she was getting dangerously near the edge of the pool, but I didn't say anything. I was too interested in seeing what would happen next. She took a final step, lost her balance, and hit the water with a huge splash.

"What were you saying, Justine?" Roni asked sweetly as Justine hauled herself out of the pool, her hair plastered to her face. "Something about . . . grace?"

"Shut up," Justine said, and stomped off to grab her towel.

Chapter

7

After Justine had calmed down we all went up to her room. It was in chaos. Enough clothing to open a new store was lying on every available surface. There were three half-packed trunks in the middle of the floor, and every imaginable item for the hair and face was lined up on her vanity.

"Justine!" Karen exclaimed.

"I haven't made up my mind yet what to take with me," Justine said. "It's a hard decision. I'll be away for a long time. I really want to take it all, but my father said no more than three cases. The rest has to go into storage. Actually I think I'll just throw it all away. It will be out of fashion by the time I come back anyway."

"Justine!" Karen said again, throwing me a horrified glance. It's hard for people like us, who have no money to spare, to understand how anyone could think like Justine.

"All that stuff over there is No Go," Justine said, waving her arms at a huge pile. "I'm sure we can find Lacey something fashionable to wear . . . although you are a little bigger than me, Lacey."

I thought this was tactful of Justine, for once. Lacey was a lot bigger than any of us. She was a big girl, tall, big boned, and strong. I picked up one of Justine's tiny denim miniskirts and giggled. "You could wear it as a hat, Lacey," I suggested.

"There is stuff here, I know it," Justine said. "See, this is an oversized top, and these are the wide-legged pants from the time I skinned my leg." She started hurling things in Lacey's direction. "And T-shirts fit anybody. I always buy mine large. Here, Lacey. Try some of this on."

"But I can't—" Lacey began.

"Sure you can," Justine said. "It will only go to the Salvation Army if you don't take it."

Lacey disappeared into the bathroom. "It will take more than just dressing her differently," Roni said quietly.

"I know. Her hair and skin are a mess," Justine agreed.

"I didn't mean that," Roni said. "I meant the way she acts."

"You're right," I said. "You can't go around slapping people on the back and saying y'all to kids at Alta Mesa. And I've got a horrible feeling that she'll cling to me like a leech."

"We have to save Ginger," Roni said to the other two. "Can you imagine what Lacey will do to her image? And she'll need to make new friends now that we're not going to be there."

"Don't talk about it." I sighed. "It's too depressing."

"This really might be our last sleepover," Karen agreed. "It's all happening too fast."

"We've still got Labor Day weekend," Roni said. "Maybe we could plan to do something together, go somewhere fun."

"Like where?"

"I don't know. Camping?"

"That would be great," I said. "Do you think our folks would let us go alone overnight?"

"Probably not," Karen said. "Not mine, anyway."

"Maybe my dad would pay for us to go to a resort in the mountains," Justine suggested.

"Justine, you can't keep expecting your dad to pay for things," I said. "He's got to pay to ship all this stuff to England."

"I think camping sounds like more fun anyway," Roni said. "Let's look into it. I really want to do something fun this weekend."

"Me too," I agreed.

The bathroom door opened and Lacey came out. In Justine's clothes she already looked like a different person. Her hair was still wet from the pool and hung limp around her shoulders, which was one step better than those braids.

"Wow, Lacey, way to go," Roni said.

"Looks good on you," Karen agreed.

"Really?" Lacey blushed bright red again.

"That's the next thing," Justine said.

"What is?"

"You have to stop blushing every time someone speaks to you."

"How do I manage that?" Lacey stammered. "I don't mean to blush. It just happens."

"You have to say to yourself: I am cool, I am confident, I am in command of myself. It always works for me," Justine said. "I just tell myself these people are lucky to be talking to me."

Roni and I grinned at each other.

"I don't think I could do that," Lacey said. "I was even kind of awkward at my old school, where I knew everybody. Now I'll be feeling like a fish out of water anyway. I won't dare say a word to anybody, and if they speak to me, I'll just die."

"We'll teach you some things to say," Roni said. "Like Henry Higgins and Eliza Doolittle."

"Do they go to your school?" Lacey asked.

This time we tried hard not to laugh.

"No, they're in a play, Lacey," Roni said. "*My Fair Lady*. Okay, rule number one. Don't ask any questions unless you're pretty sure you know the answer. We don't want any repetitions of Paris, Texas."

"And you have to learn not to touch people all the time, Lacey," I added. "You can hug your friends, when you make friends, but here you don't grab people and you don't slap them on the back or nudge them or push them all the time."

"I know." Lacey sighed. "I got in trouble for that back home too. The girls at my old school used to say I acted more like a boy than a girl."

"Why don't you keep your hands in your pockets when you're talking to new people, Lacey?" Karen suggested. "Or take a pocketbook with you and hold onto it."

"She'd probably slug them with the pocketbook," I commented.

"I think we have to practice this," Justine said. "Follow me, Lacey." She walked across the room with a model's graceful slink. When she drew level with Karen, she held out her hand. "Hi there, I'm Lacey from Texas. I'm new here. So nice to meet you," she said in a low, sexy voice. "Now you try it," she said to Lacey.

Lacey tried. The first five times she had to stop because we were laughing so much, but by the sixth she didn't sound or look bad.

"That's all you say for the first few days, except for yes and no," Justine said. "That way you won't risk putting your foot in your mouth."

"I don't think . . ."

"Don't worry about a thing, Lacey," Justine said. "This is the last assignment for the Boyfriend Club before we all split up: to get Lacey ready for Alta Mesa in a week."

"The Boyfriend Club? What's that?" Lacey asked.

"It's a joke," I said hastily.

"No, it's not," Karen said. "It started as a joke, but it turned into a good idea. When one of us needs help meeting a guy, we put our heads together. Then we snoop around and help get the girl and guy together."

"What a great idea," Lacey yelled, jumping up excitedly. "Y'all can do it for me! I sure need the help. I never had a boyfriend—'cept Bubba Benson, and he didn't count 'cause his dad said he had to take me to the freshman dance or he didn't get to drive the truck. Do you think your club could come up with a guy for me?"

"It never really worked that well for us, Lacey," I said quickly. "Something always seemed to go wrong."

"But we were great at makeovers, right?" Roni said. She was playing with Lacey's hair, eyeing it critically.

"And we all found cute guys," Karen pointed out.

"And lost them again," Justine reminded her. "Except for Ginger."

"And we—" I began. Suddenly Roni and Lacey shrieked.

Roni was standing over Lacey, holding a large chunk of Lacey's hair in her hand. "I-I didn't mean it," she stammered. "I was just wondering how she'd look with short hair. I didn't realize the scissors were sharp."

Lacey put her hand to her head. "Gol-lee," she wailed. "What am I going to do? My mom will kill me. She just loved all that long hair."

"I'm sorry," Roni said again. "It was an accident. Your mom will understand that, won't she? They don't shoot people for cutting hair where you come from, do they?"

Lacey started to laugh. "There ain't much we can

do about it now," she said, turning her head from side to side as she examined herself in the mirror. "I guess y'all better go ahead and snip off the rest. That way my mom can't say too much except what's done is done."

"It worked for me," Roni said, "but if you really liked having long hair . . ."

"Liked it? It was the ugliest thing I ever saw," Lacey said. "It's just that Mama was so set on long braids." She shook her head again. "I think I like it better already. Get cutting, Roni."

Half an hour later Lacey had a shoulder-length bob. It made her look entirely different, and she was delighted. "First step in the new me," she said. "Now y'all have to teach me how to act."

"We've got a long night ahead of us," Justine said dryly.

The next morning, I got home just in time to hear the phone ring. It was Fred Cochran, one of Dad's fishing buddies. "Just wanted to let him know that I won't be using the cabin this weekend if he wants it," he said.

"Okay, I'll tell him," I answered.

"Tell me what?" Dad asked, coming in from the garage.

"Fred says you can have his cabin this weekend if you want," I said, covering the mouthpiece.

"That's too bad," Dad said. "I can't really go, not with your uncle and aunt to entertain. Tell Fred thanks anyway."

I was about to speak when I got the most perfect idea. "Can we have the cabin, Dad?" I asked. "Me and my friends? It'll be our last time together."

"I don't see why not," Dad said, "if it's okay with Fred."

Fred said it was just fine with him. I hung up the phone and threw my arms around Dad. "I'm so lucky to have a father like you," I said.

"Remember, you have to include your cousin, too," Dad said.

"I already was," I assured him. An added bonus of two days away was that we'd have time to work on Lacey. With any luck the girl who came with me to Alta Mesa on Tuesday morning would not slap people on the back and yell "Gol-lee" in their faces!

Chapter

8

I couldn't wait to call Roni and the others. They were all as excited as I was about the cabin. Then I rushed straight to the garage and dragged out the sleeping bags.

"What are you doing with that stuff?" Todd asked, coming in with Ben behind him.

"Going up to Fred's cabin this weekend," I said.

"With Dad?"

"By ourselves. Just me and Roni and my friends."

"No way," Todd said. "Dad would never let you go alone."

"He already said okay."

"You can't be serious," Todd exploded. He looked at Ben for support. "He can't let a bunch of girls go up to a cabin alone. What was he thinking?"

"For your information, we are quite able to look after ourselves," I said. "Mr. Ruiz is going to drive us up and Dad will come get us. It's all arranged."

"Well, you can't take those sleeping bags," Todd said. "I need them—we're going camping with some of the guys."

"Alone?"

"Of course."

"What was Dad thinking, letting a bunch of little boys go camping alone?" I teased.

"I can see Todd's point, Ginger," Ben said carefully. "I mean, you girls, alone in the mountains?"

"It's forty miles from Phoenix, for crying out loud," I said, rolling my eyes up to the ceiling, "not in the middle of Alaska."

"But what if something happens to you? What if there are strangers prowling around?"

"There are five of us," I said, "and we're not exactly babies. Besides, Fred's cabin is safe enough. I've been there before."

"I still don't like it," Ben said. "I've got an idea, Todd. Why don't we go camping with them? Then we can keep an eye on them."

"No way!" I exclaimed.

Ben looked hurt. "You don't want me around?"

"Of course I want you around, but not this week-end," I said.

He was pouting. "You don't think it would be romantic up in the mountains, under the stars?".

"It could be very romantic," I said slowly, "but this is the last weekend before all my friends go in different directions. We might never have another chance like this. That's why it has to be just us, and no outsiders."

"Okay, I guess," Ben said, "but I'm not very happy about this. It's dangerous up in the mountains. What if you stumble across a cougar or a rattlesnake?"

"What if you do? You're going camping too."

"We're men," Todd said. "We can defend ourselves."

"That's ridiculous. We can defend ourselves too," I said. "And if you try to change Dad's mind, Todd Hartman, I'll tell him about the time you borrowed his chain saw and—"

"You wouldn't dare!"

"I would," I said sweetly. "So be a nice brother. You go camping with your friends and I'll go to the cabin with mine."

"Okay, but you're not taking my sleeping bag," Todd said.

"Don't worry. I'll just take my own. I'm sure

Lacey's used to sleeping in the straw," I commented.

On Saturday morning, Lacey showed up with a big canvas bag. "It's my sleeping bag," she said. "It belonged to my dad."

"I just hope there's room in the car," I said. "Who knows what Justine will bring with her."

The Mercedes pulled up a few minutes later and Justine stepped out, carrying one small backpack.

"Bye," she called, waving to her stepmother. "See you Sunday night."

"Justine, it's a miracle," I called, running to meet her.

"What is?"

"You going anywhere with only that amount of luggage."

The Mercedes had begun to drive away.

"Luggage?" Justine shrieked. "Oh my gosh, I forgot my luggage in the trunk. Wait, Christine! Don't go!" She started to run after the car.

"I knew it was too good to be true," I said as I went to help her carry her three suitcases into the driveway.

"I don't know what came over me," Justine said. "I guess I was thinking too much about leaving you guys and going to England."

"It won't be forever, Justine."

"It will feel like forever," she said. "By the time I come back we'll all have grown up and changed. You'll have different friends and be doing different things. Maybe we won't like each other anymore."

"Of course we will," I said.

Roni's car pulled up. She climbed out and stood staring at Justine's pile of luggage. "You're going to have to leave some of this behind, Justine," she said.

"But I can't. I need it all."

"I'll put it this way," Roni said. "Either you can go, or all your luggage can go, but not both."

"Meany," Justine said. "Well, I suppose I could do without my CD player for one weekend. And there probably won't be a fancy restaurant close by where we'd be likely to go for dinner, so I can leave that bag of formal clothes. . . ."

Roni looked at me and shook her head. "Justine, you're really something else," she said.

"I can't help it if I like to be prepared." Justine sniffed. "You wait until we meet some cute boys and they invite us to go waterskiing and I'm the only one with a life jacket."

"There isn't even a lake," I said, laughing.

"But you said your dad goes fishing."

"There's a creek with a swimming hole," I said.

"So? We might meet some guys with a car *and* a boat and they'd drive us to the nearest lake," she said smugly. "And I'll be prepared."

We stuffed as much of Justine's stuff as possible into the station wagon and headed over to Karen's house. Of course, she only had one tiny bag. After Karen had climbed into the backseat with us, we headed up into the mountains.

The day was bright and clear and the trees glowed green against a deep blue sky. The air began to smell fresh and piney. We were all excited as Mr. Ruiz left the paved road and we bumped down a dusty track to the cabin. We tumbled out gratefully, stiff from being crammed in like sardines for so long.

"So here's the cabin," Karen said excitedly. "It is so cute."

"It is so primitive," Justine said. "Don't tell me that's an outhouse over there. Don't tell me there's no indoor plumbing."

"'Fraid so," I said. "I did warn you it wasn't fancy."

But as I looked at the cabin now, I realized I had forgotten just how un-fancy it was.

"I'm sure it will be very nice," Karen said, picking up her bag with a smile.

"Are you girls sure you'll be okay?" Mr. Ruiz said, looking around. "I hadn't realized how isolated you would be. Are there other houses nearby?"

"Only back on the main road."

"And you don't have a phone?"

"No electricity."

"No electricity!" Justine wailed. "But what about my hair dryer? How will I dry my hair?"

"You won't want to wash it, because there's only cold water," I said.

"Not wash my hair? Are you crazy? I'll feel yucky."

"It's for one night, Justine," I said.

Justine made a face. "Okay. I'll try to rough it," she said. "Let's go take a look."

I turned the key in the lock. The door opened with a sort of horror-movie creak. It was very dark inside. A weak beam of sunlight came through the shutters on the window. The place looked as if nobody had been there for years. There was thick dust on the floor, a rickety bed in the corner, and an old table next to the potbellied stove.

"Let's get this place opened up," Roni said, coughing as our feet stirred up the dust. She walked over to open the window and screamed. "There's a giant spider!" she cried. "And it's looking right at me!"

Lacey started to laugh. "Don't tell me y'all are scared of a little old spider," she said. "Shoot, we had hundreds of spiders at home. I'll get rid of it for you." She picked up a stick and started attacking the cobweb.

"Lacey, you're so brave," Karen said. "When you've done the window, would you come over here? There are spiderwebs all over the bed."

"I think I'll sleep on the floor," Roni said quickly.

"I might sleep outside," I said.

"Y'all are a bunch of scaredy cats," Lacey said. "Reminds me of them chickens, Cousin Ginger."

"What chickens?" Justine asked.

"Lacey, shut up," I began, but she kept on anyway, laughing loudly. "Cousin Ginger here went to feed the chickens and she said they attacked her. You should have seen her—she ran a mile! You'd have thought she had a great big bear coming after her."

"They were fierce chickens," I said lamely. My friends were all grinning.

All through lunch, Lacey kept telling stories to embarrass me and amuse my friends. They seemed to think she was incredibly funny. I stood apart, watching them all laughing together. Why did they find Lacey's stories funny when I found them annoying? Maybe because they hadn't had to share a room with her for a month. And they hadn't had to put up with her laughing at them each time they made a dumb mistake.

"We'll need wood for the barbecue," I said. Nobody answered me, so I just wandered off. It felt good to be alone in the stillness of the mountains. I walked farther and farther, collecting a big armful of firewood.

"Okay, dinner's taken care of," I called as I came back to the cabin. "This should be enough wood to keep us going."

"Oh, Ginger, you didn't have to do that," Karen said. "Lacey found the ax and she's already chopped the firewood that was stored here."

"She's so strong," Roni said. "We told her she should run for Miss Atlas and she said she didn't know that much about geography. Isn't she a riot?"

"Oh, sure," I said. "A real riot."

"What's eating you?" Roni asked.

"Nothing. I guess I'm just depressed."

"At least you've got Lacey to make you laugh," Roni said. "Her stories are so funny, Ginger. I still hurt from laughing. I thought she was going to be a real pain from your description."

"You haven't had a chance to see her annoying side yet," I commented, dumping my useless firewood on the ground. Lacey got the fire going and we cooked hot dogs and corn on the cob. They tasted the way only food cooked outdoors can taste.

Afterward we sat back, content, leaning against the warm rocks to watch the sunset.

"In ten more days I'll be in cold, rainy England," Justine said.

"In three more days I'll be at the conservatory, with five hours of violin practice a day."

"And I'll be dodging spitballs from all those creeps at Oak Creek," Roni said.

I wanted to say, "And I'll be all alone at Alta Mesa, stuck with Lacey." But I didn't.

"I wish we'd brought a video camera," Karen said. "I'd love to keep remembering how pretty it is tonight and how good it feels to be with my friends."

"Did someone say video camera?" Justine asked. "Why didn't you guys remind me?" She rushed into the cabin and reappeared with a brand-new video camera. "I bought it to go to England," she said. "And I remembered to throw it in my bag at the last minute. Okay, smile. Say something funny."

"Something funny!" we all yelled at the same time.

We were still hamming it up for the camera when we heard a noise in the bushes.

"What was that?" Karen asked, spinning around.

"Just an animal," I said. I noticed that it had suddenly become quite dark.

"Sounded like a pretty big animal," Justine said nervously.

"Do they have mountain lions up here?" Lacey asked. I noticed that even *she* didn't sound brave any longer.

I nodded. "But a mountain lion would never attack five people at once . . . I don't think."

"Let's go in the cabin," Karen said.

We didn't need telling twice. We all ran inside and barred the door.

"Maybe we can see it from the window," Roni suggested. "Stand very still and don't make any noise."

"What if it tries to jump in through the window?" Karen whispered.

"It won't," I said, hoping I was right.

We stood there, holding our breath. Outside, in the growing darkness, we could definitely hear the progress of some large animal. A twig snapped close to the house and then there was a low growl. Lacey grabbed my arm. "Is there a gun in the cabin, Cousin Ginger?" she whispered.

"You're not going to shoot anything, Lacey," I said firmly.

Then Karen grabbed my other arm. "It's not an animal, it's a person," she whispered. "Look, see the blue shirt?"

103

"So it's a hiker just passing by this way." I tried to sound casual.

"Then why is he creeping through the bushes like that?" Roni hissed. "I don't like it, Ginger. Shut the window and lock it."

"You guys are freaking out over nothing," I said. "I think we should just go outside and say hi to him. He'll see there are five of us. . . ."

"I wonder if I still remember karate," Justine said thoughtfully. "I can't remember what color belt I got up to. Pink, I think, or was it brown? I remember I didn't like the shade, so I asked if I could skip it and go straight to black. Black is always so basic, don't you think?"

"Justine, shut up," Roni and I said at the same time. I guess we were all a little edgy.

"Well, let's go confront him, if we're going," Roni said. She headed for the door. I was right beside her. We stopped in the doorway and peered into the evening twilight.

"Hi," I called. "Do you need help?"

There was a rapid movement of blue shirt in the bushes, but nobody appeared. Then there was a flash of white beside it.

"There's more than one of them," Justine whispered. "What are we going to do now?"

"I'll tell you what," Lacey yelled, holding up a broomstick. "This here's a shotgun I've got in my hands and I ain't afraid to use it. I don't know what you're doing in them bushes, but come out of there right now with your hands up."

"Lacey!" I exclaimed in horror. But before I could do anything sensible the bushes parted. A large shape emerged.

"Don't shoot!" Ben said.

Chapter 9

"Ben Campbell, do you mind telling me what you think you're doing here?" I demanded. I was still scared, so I sounded even madder than I really was.

"Todd's with me," he said sheepishly. Todd scrambled out of the bushes behind him.

"Hi," he said.

"Don't you hi me," I snapped. "You were spying on us!"

"Not really spying," Todd said. "Just checking to make sure everything was okay up here."

"We saw smoke," Ben added.

"Yeah, from the barbecue! We just had dinner, okay?"

"Ben was worried about you," Todd said.

"Aw, how sweet," Roni said.

I dug her in the side. "Shut up," I said. "It isn't sweet at all. It's insulting. Ben still thinks I'm a little kid who can't take care of herself."

"I didn't realize you had a hired gun," Ben said with a grin as he looked at Lacey.

Lacey blushed and looked embarrassed. "It wasn't really a gun," she said. "I just wanted to scare whoever it was."

"It worked," Ben admitted.

"Sure did," Todd said. "I wasn't sure whether to come out or run away and risk getting shotgun pellets in my rear end."

"So you decided to camp near here?" I asked.

"Down by the creek," Ben said. "It's a nice spot."

"You left your buddies down there?"

"They didn't come," Todd said. "It's just Ben and me."

"Just the two of you? All alone? In a tent?" I asked, giving Roni a knowing smile. "I don't think that's very safe, do you, Roni?"

"No way," Roni said. "We'd better sneak down and keep an eye on them."

"Well, thanks for your concern, guys," I said. "As you can see, we're all fine. So go back to your tent and leave us alone."

"Were you planning to have a campfire?" Todd asked.

"We hadn't thought about it. Sounds like a good idea," I said.

"That's what we thought, too," Todd said, "but there are no open fires allowed this time of year in the state campground, where we are. We've got all the stuff to make s'mores and nowhere to make them."

"I love s'mores," Roni said.

"So do I," Karen and Justine agreed.

"You guys could build up the fire in the barbecue pit," Todd suggested.

"We could, Ginger," Karen said.

"Lacey can cut us some more wood," Justine suggested. "I mean s'more wood!"

"And we could run back down to the campsite and bring up the candy bars and the graham crackers and marshmallows," Ben said.

Everyone was looking at me as though I was the camp counselor. "Oh, why not," I grumbled.

A couple of hours later we sat around the barbecue pit, watching the sparks dance upward to the stars.

"I'm so full I'm going to burst," Lacey moaned.

"If anyone ever shows me a marshmallow again, I'll scream," Justine agreed.

"Don't worry, Justine. I bet they don't have s'mores in England," Roni said.

"Come look at the stars, Ginger," Ben whispered, pulling me to my feet. I saw Roni nudge Karen and I made a face at them. Ben took my hand and we walked out of the circle of firelight.

"See how close the stars look," Ben said.

It was true. They were so big and bright that they seemed to be hanging just above our heads.

"They look like you could just reach up and grab one," I said.

"I'd grab one for you if I could," Ben said.

"Ben . . ." I looked up at him. "Sometimes you say the sweetest things. Sometimes you are so annoying that you drive me crazy, but then—"

"But then I make up for it?" he whispered. He slid his arms around me and pulled me close to him.

"More than make up for it," I whispered back. I lifted my face. His lips were warm and still tasted of chocolate and marshmallow as they met mine.

The boys hadn't been gone long when we heard the first distant rumble. We all sat up in our sleeping bags.

"What's that?" Karen whispered.

"Thunder?" I suggested. There was a flash of lightning and another rumble.

"Sounds like it's heading this way," Lacey said calmly. I glared at her in the darkness. She was already taking up most of the floor with her oversized army surplus sleeping bag.

Then I remembered something. "Ben and Todd are down there in a tent," I said. "I hope they're going to be okay."

"Maybe it will just be one of those quick little summer storms," Roni said.

Immediately there was a downpour. It was as if someone had turned on a giant faucet in the sky. The rain hammered on the roof so hard that it sounded like a herd of stampeding cattle was running over us.

"Then again, maybe it won't be just a little summer storm," Roni added.

It didn't take long to find out that the roof leaked. First it dripped on Karen, then on me, then on Justine, who let out a yell loud enough to wake Phoenix. Then it did more than drip. In the end only Lacey's giant sleeping bag was still dry.

"Let's put it up on the bed and we can all get in it," I suggested.

"There's not room for y'all," Lacey complained.

"Too bad, everywhere else is wet," I said. We huddled together, feeling cold and miserable while the drops fell around us. Lightning lit up the room and was followed almost immediately by a clap of thunder that shook the whole cabin. Roni grabbed me.

The storm went on and on. Finally the whole roof was leaking except for one tiny corner, where we huddled together, jumping and clutching each other every time there was another flash and crash.

"We're really high up here," Karen said shakily. "Do cabins get struck by lightning?"

"There are trees around," Roni said, trying to sound brave. "It would strike a tree first."

"Then travel along the ground to the cabin?" Justine wailed. "And we've got that iron stove in the corner. Is iron a good conductor?"

"Y'all sure make a big fuss about things," Lacey said. "Shoot, we get storms like this almost every day in summer."

I ignored her. "I hope Todd and Ben are okay," I whispered to Roni.

"Don't worry. They'll be fine," Roni said. "It's not like it's the first time they've been camping. They know what to do."

At last the lightning died to distant flickers and the thunder rumbled away, but we still didn't get much sleep. The roof kept on dripping, and everywhere was wet, except for Lacey's sleeping bag. We huddled together like a litter of puppies. I've never been so glad to see morning.

Outside, there were pine needles everywhere and small branches lying around, but no signs of the real strength of the storm. The sky was clear and light blue. It was going to be another beautiful day.

"Okay, who wants pancakes?" Lacey asked. "I'll get the fire going, if I can find enough dry wood."

"I think I'll go down and see how the boys are first," I said.

"We'll come with you," Karen offered.

We made our way down the hill. It wasn't easy going. The rain had gouged out great chunks of the trail and thrown branches across it. My heart was beating faster and faster. "They're okay," I kept telling myself. "They're not stupid. They know how to take care of themselves."

Then we reached the bottom of the valley. What had been a tiny creek yesterday was now an angry torrent that came cascading into the valley like Niagara Falls. There was no sign of a campsite or a tent. Then Roni touched my arm and pointed to a cooking pot lying upside down on the muddy banks of the new river.

"Oh no," I gasped. I started to run forward. "Ben? Todd? Where are you?" I screamed.

"Ginger?" A voice echoed out of the roar of the waters.

"Where are you?" I yelled again.

"Up here, in the tree."

A large oak tree stood in what was now the middle of the stream. I spotted a hand waving from the branches.

"Are you okay?" I screamed.

"We're stuck up here," Ben's voice came back. "Go get a ranger or somebody!"

"Hold on a second," Lacey yelled. "I saw some rope up at the cabin. I'll be right back."

Roni gave me a questioning look as Lacey ran back up the hill. I shrugged.

"What happened to your tent?" Justine yelled.

"Gone. The water took everything," Ben yelled back. "We were lucky it didn't take us."

Lacey appeared again, carrying a big coil of rope. "Y'all are lucky that I won the first prize in the lassoing contest," she yelled. "Try to grab onto the rope when I throw it."

She arranged the rope in her hands and then flung it in the direction of the boys. The first time it hit the trunk and dropped into the water. Lacey drew it back in and recoiled it. The next time Ben's hand shot out and grabbed it.

We cheered.

"I'm not a wide receiver for nothing," Ben called. "What do we do now?"

"Tie it around a solid branch," Lacey instructed. "One that can take your weight. And don't tie a granny knot, okay?"

"Okay."

"Now we're going to hold tight to the other end and y'all can slide down. One at a time, mind. We can't take both your weight."

I held my breath as first Todd and then Ben climbed down the rope over the churning, frothing water. When they were safely on dry land we all hugged and laughed and cried at the same time.

"Boy, am I glad you brought Cousin Lacey with you, Ginger," Todd said.

"Yeah, Lacey, you're amazing," Ben said. "I've never seen anyone throw a rope like that."

As usual, Lacey blushed. "I'm just glad that my little country skills come in handy once in a while," she said. "Now y'all better come up to the cabin and get dried off. I'll make y'all pancakes."

I could tell that everyone else thought Lacey was pretty incredible. I suppose I did too. I knew I couldn't have thrown a rope like that, or chopped the wood, but it really bugged me. I'd assumed that Lacey would be the outsider here in Phoenix, and I'd look good in comparison. But it didn't seem to be working out that way. Was I destined always to have Lacey get the better of me?

After breakfast the boys hiked off to see if their truck was okay in the parking lot and we spent a lazy day in the sun. It was hard to believe there had been a storm last night. We were almost sorry when it came time to pack up and wait for my dad.

"Come and stand together," Karen called, waving her camera at us. "I want to have a memory of this."

"And I'll get it on video," Justine said.

We tried to clown around, but it wasn't easy.

"This really is good-bye, isn't it?" Roni said softly. "In a couple of days we all go in different directions."

"I'll never forget you guys, never," Justine said. Tears started to trickle down her cheeks.

"Don't, Justine. You're making me cry," Karen said. "I'll never forget you guys either."

"We'll get together," I said, but I was crying too. "We'll do things on weekends."

"But it won't be the same," Roni said.

"Cut it out, y'all," Lacey said. "I don't hardly know you guys, but you're making me cry too."

We looked up at the sound of a vehicle approaching. My dad stared in surprise at five tear-stained faces.

"What's been going on here?" he asked. "Didn't you have a good time?"

"A wonderful time," I sobbed. "We don't want it to end."

Chapter

10

I opened my eyes to cold dawn light and wondered
for a second why my stomach was tying itself in
knots. Then I remembered. It was really here. The
first day of school, with no Roni, no Karen, no
Justine—and more Lacey than I ever wanted. I
pulled my quilt over my head and wondered if I
really had to go to school today. Maybe I could con-
vince my dad I was sick.

I kicked off the covers with a sigh and dragged
myself to the bathroom. Then I carefully pulled out
my new "first day of school" outfit—linen walking
shorts, a dark brown tank top with beige trim, *and* a
brown scrunchie. See, I was coordinated enough to
please even Justine. And I didn't care. It didn't seem

to matter anymore. Justine wouldn't be there to see.

I'd just finished making my lunch when Lacey walked right in without knocking.

"Hi, Cuz, ready to roll?" she asked. "I don't want to be late on my first morning."

"Chill, Lacey," I said. "We have oodles of time."

"So?" she asked, staring hard at me. "How do I look?"

"Fine," I said.

"Really, truly?"

"Sure, you look fine," I said. Actually she looked a lot better than I ever thought she would. Her hair, now shoulder length, thanks to Roni and the wandering scissors, had become quite curly. She was wearing it loose, and it made her face look softer. She was also wearing Justine's wide-leg pants and a white shirt. I wouldn't have recognized her as the farm girl who was throwing around bales of hay in overalls a month ago.

"Let's go," she said. "I am so nervous. I just hope I make it to school before I need to go to the bathroom again. They don't have bathrooms on buses, do they?"

"No, they don't," I said, wondering if this was one more thing she was about to embarrass me with. "You'd better go once more before we leave."

"No time," she said, consulting her watch. "Just pray the bus doesn't get stuck in a traffic jam."

I gave a loud, weary sigh as I closed the door behind us. "Sophomore year, here we come," I said to myself.

While we were standing at the bus stop, a yellow school bus rattled past. I looked up to see Roni waving crazily at me. "Help," she mouthed, pointing to a couple of creepy guys who were grinning at me from the seat in front of her. Poor Roni, she'd had so many hopes and dreams for this year! I bet there wouldn't be a musical at Oak Creek, or a debate team, or any of the other things she'd planned to do.

The city bus arrived and we headed in the other direction, into the middle of town. I remembered so clearly the first time Roni and I had ridden the bus together. We'd been terrified and hopeful at the same time. And we had both totally freaked out when we saw our school with all three thousand kids hanging around the front gates.

That was exactly what Lacey did. I climbed from the bus, looking out for faces I knew. Lacey grabbed me so hard that I was jerked backward.

"Lacey!" I yelled. "Would you let go of me!"

"Shoot, Ginger, look at all those people," she gasped. "I can't go in there. I just can't do it. I don't belong here."

She was still holding my arm as if it was a lifeline and she was drowning. This was about to turn into a most embarrassing entrance. "You'll be fine, Lacey," I hissed. "Please let go of me. You're ripping my shirt and you're embarrassing me."

"Hi, Ginger!" someone yelled.

I recognized some kids from the track team.

"Hey, how's it going?" I yelled back. I shook Lacey free with all my strength so that I could wave.

"Where's Roni?" someone else yelled.

"Not here. She had to transfer."

"Transfer? That's too bad. Who's going to run the eight hundred this year?"

"We'll save you a place in line, Ginger," another girl in the group yelled as they began to fight their way through the crowd.

"Thanks," I yelled back.

We had reached the main gate where the crowd was thickest. Lacey grabbed onto me again. "Don't lose me, Ginger," she pleaded. "Just don't let go of me."

We fought our way toward the gym, where freshmen and sophomores had to pick up their class schedules. And suddenly it seemed as if I knew everybody I passed.

"Yo, Ginger, how's it going? Where's Roni? Are

you joining the ecology club this fall? Are you going out for cross-country? Are you and Ben still an item?"

Suddenly it hit me, in a great rush of warmth. This was my school. I belonged here. People knew me. I made my way across the quad, yelling answers to questions and greeting people like old friends, even if I'd only sat behind them in class last year.

By the time I got to the schedule line, I must have answered the Roni, Karen, and Justine question a zillion times. And almost a zillion people must have said, "You can eat lunch with us if you want. You know where we always sit."

I began to feel better by the minute—or I would have if Lacey wasn't still hanging onto the strap of my backpack.

"Lacey, you have to wait on the other side of the gym," I told her impatiently. "That's where the freshmen schedules are."

But she refused to go alone. Instead I had to wait on two lines—one for my schedule and one for hers. *Great*, I thought. *At this rate she'll be clinging to me for the whole year*. I was really glad, when we finally picked up our class schedules, to discover that the only class we had together was PE. Thank goodness Lacey was only a freshman! With any luck, she'd make some friends in her classes and stay out of my hair.

I delivered her to the door of Spanish 1.

"Don't go, Ginger," she said, grabbing me again.

"I have to. I have world history clean across campus."

"But I don't know anybody. I won't know what to do. What if they can all speak Spanish?"

"They can't. That's why it's called Spanish 1. You'll be fine. If you can't find your way, just ask. There are a zillion new freshmen today who can't find their way either. I'll see you in PE, right before lunch. You can't miss the gym. It's where we got our schedules."

"Okay," she whimpered. "I wish I could have gone to Oak Creek with Roni. I'd have done just fine there."

I thought about Roni as I hurried to my own first class. I just hoped they hadn't put her next to Joe Garcia, who was a big jerk. And hopefully she had some teachers who would actually teach her something worthwhile. Maybe it wouldn't be so bad for her. But I still wished she could be back here, with me.

I was looking forward to world history. We had Mr. Levitan, who was supposed to be one of the best teachers in the school. And when I went into the classroom, I saw that we had a lot of the best kids, too. There were no idiots or goof-offs, and I wondered if I was in the right classroom. There were a couple of nerds, of course. Owen was there, wearing a dark sports jacket, even though the temperature outside was way over a hundred. His hair no longer stood up in spikes on top of his head but was parted to one side and slicked down, making him look like the world's youngest politician. Next to him was another nerd I hadn't seen before. He wore big glasses and his hair flopped forward across his face, so that he had to keep shaking it back.

"Ginger!" Owen called. "Good to see you. I'd like you to meet Jeremy Rosenberg, who just transferred here. His locker is next to mine, so I decided I'd better show him the ropes. Jeremy, this is my good friend Ginger Hartman."

Jeremy blushed scarlet. "Pleased to meet you," he muttered, his eyes not meeting mine.

"Come sit here," Owen said, indicating a seat beside him and grinning at me. The repulsive grin was one of the things that hadn't changed about him. And he was still annoying. That hadn't changed either.

I looked around frantically, trying to think of an excuse not to sit next to Owen. Josh White caught my eye. He was sitting over by the window.

"I've already saved Ginger a seat over here," he called. "Get over here, Ginger, before someone takes it."

I didn't need any encouragement. "Thanks," I muttered as I slid into the seat behind Josh. "You saved me from . . ."

"A fate worse than death?" Josh asked, his eyes flickering in amusement.

"No kidding," I agreed.

He swiveled around in his seat, resting his arm on the back of his chair. "Did you ever wonder why they don't make a magnet school for nerds?" he asked in a low voice. "They'd love it. Sci-fi posters on all the walls, all classes on the Internet, a bookstore that sells mouse pads in assorted colors . . ."

"And a varsity Nintendo squad?" I suggested. It was amazing—his brain was running on exactly the same wavelength as mine! I had even discussed this subject with my friends.

His face lit up and he laughed. He had a wonderful laugh, the kind that made you start smiling too. Josh was that kind of person. He was one of those totally confident people who expect everybody to like them, so everybody does. He'd been elected sophomore class treasurer for this year. We'd wondered why he didn't run for president, because he would have gotten it, but he'd claimed he liked handling the money. And also Don Pritchard had set his heart on being president, as a logical step en route to the White House. Don and Josh had been best friends last year, and I always suspected that Josh hadn't wanted to run against his buddy.

I looked around the room. "What happened to Don?" I asked.

"Didn't you hear? His family moved over the summer. His dad got a job in Washington, D.C., and they just up and went. Now he's in his element, of course. He's already applying for internships with Congress."

"So what happens about class president? Does the vice president take over?"

"Amy Schmidt? Are you crazy? What could she ever preside over? She only got the job because she ran unopposed."

"So why don't you do it?"

"No thanks. I don't have the time," he said. "I have to get an after-school job this year. Treasurer suits me fine. Anyway, they're going to have a new election for pres. Mr. Levitan told me."

Mr. Levitan came into the classroom then, and Josh turned to face forward. I found that I was grinning to myself. Making friends with Josh White on the first day of school was definitely a plus.

At lunchtime there was a welcome rally in the quad. Lacey was still clinging to me, so I dragged her along.

"What's this all about?" she asked.

"It's supposed to be about school spirit," I said. "They do cheers and the band plays and there are always fun stunts and games."

"Y'all have cheerleaders," Lacey said, her face lighting up.

"Who did you think cheered at football games?" I asked.

"I thought this school might be too fancy for stuff like cheerleaders," she said. "Those uniforms sure look pretty. Ours were so old at my school. They were supposed to be black, but they were gray."

Rich Bailey, the new commissioner of spirit, came onto the stage with a mike and introduced the varsity team and the varsity cheerleaders. The cheerleaders did a couple of cheers. "I know that one," Lacey hissed excitedly in my ear.

"And now, ladies and gentlemen," Rich said. "This is your big chance. Today's stunt—arm wrestle a football player. If you beat him, you get his place on the team! No, just kidding. You get a free pass to a home game. Okay, volunteers, please."

"Arm wrestling. I can do that," Lacey yelled. Before I could stop her, she had leaped up onto the stage. She was the only girl. I closed my eyes and prayed that nobody knew she was with me.

"What's this? We have a female challenger?" I heard Rich yelling. "All right! What's your name? Lacey! All right, Lacey, let's see an arm-wrestling champ in action!"

I noticed he had deliberately put her against one of the smallest guys on varsity, not one of the big linebackers. She gave him a bright smile, and then smashed his arm down to the table. Everyone roared.

"Okay, Lacey. On to the next challenger," Rich yelled.

Lacey looked down the line of football players. "I'll take him," she said, and pointed to Ben.

"Ben Campbell. Star wide receiver," Rich taunted. "He catches passes, but can he beat Wonder Woman?"

Lacey sat opposite Ben, so I could see her face. Her eyes were very bright as they locked onto his. Ben's back was to me, so I couldn't see if he was looking at her too. For a long time they sat still, the muscles standing out on their forearms. Then gradually Lacey's arm began to sag and Ben forced it to the table. There were cheers and jeers. "Boo, Campbell, for beating up on a girl! Save it for the Scottsdale Panthers!"

"Let's hear it for Lacey," Rich yelled. There was wild applause, screaming, and hooting. Lacey's face was bright red, but her eyes were still shining as she climbed down from the stage.

A group of cheerleaders surrounded her immediately. They were the sort of girls I stayed away from, the ones who thought they were so hot, who giggled loudly and then looked around to see who was watching them. Chrissy Peterson was among them, and she was one of the biggest snobs in my grade. She was also the biggest airhead.

"That was awesome!" Chrissy squealed. "You showed those guys they're not such studs after all." She glanced flirtatiously at the players.

Lacey smiled shyly. "I couldn't beat Ben," she said. "He was just too strong for me."

"I don't know you. Are you new?" Chrissy asked.

"I just moved here," Lacey said. "I was a cheerleader at my old school."

"That's great," Chrissy cried. "Why don't you come to tryouts after school today? We can always use good people."

Lacey came flying back to me. "I'm going to

cheerleading tryouts after school. Is that okay? Will you wait for me?"

"You want me to wait around while you go to tryouts?"

"You could try out too."

I shook my head. "No thanks. That's not my thing." I didn't admit that I'd been to tryouts last year and I'd been a total, horrible failure.

"But I don't want to ride the bus home alone," Lacey whimpered. I noticed that she only whimpered when she couldn't get her own way. "Your dad wanted you to keep an eye on me. How will I know the right bus? Please stay, just today? Please?"

"Okay, I guess," I said, "but don't get your hopes up too high. The cheerleading squad is pretty good here. They can do all the tumbling moves and most of them have taken gymnastics. I just wouldn't want you to be disappointed."

"That nice girl Chrissy did invite me," Lacey said. "She was real friendly, wasn't she, Ginger? You have nice kids here at this school. I think I'm going to like it after all."

I wasn't mean enough to say anything to burst her bubble. So after school Lacey bounced off to cheerleading tryouts and I sat in the shade on the front steps. There was no way I was going to watch her. As the school yard was emptying out, I looked up and caught my breath. I thought I was seeing a ghost. Justine ran across the parking lot toward me.

"Justine, what are you doing here?" I asked.

"I thought I'd visit one last time," Justine said. She came to sit beside me. "I live close by, after all. How was the first day?"

"Not bad," I said. "I've got good classes and people have been really nice to me. Now if I could just get rid of Lacey . . ."

"Looks like you have."

"She's at cheerleading tryouts."

"No way! Did you warn her what those girls are like?"

"I tried to. She wouldn't listen."

"She's going to make a big fool of herself," Justine said.

"Are you excited about going to England?" I asked. I was sick of thinking about Lacey.

Justine sighed. "I'm having major second thoughts," she admitted. "My dad found me a school. It's called Saint Acne, or something like that, and it's really, really old, and they wear red uniforms, and it's all girls. Can you imagine? You know I look terrible in red. I tried to talk him out of it over the phone, but he said it's where all the princes and dukes send their daughters."

"Maybe it won't be so bad when you get there."

"Huh," she said. "Maybe it will be worse. This whole thing isn't fair, Ginger. There should be a teenagers' rights campaign. We shouldn't be dragged around like luggage when we don't want to go."

"I thought you were looking forward to England."

"I was. But now I'm not," she said. Suddenly she gasped. "Oh my gosh, it's the nerds. Don't move and they won't see us."

The nerd pack moved across the parking lot to the gate.

"Owen looks almost civilized these days," Justine commented. "And who's that with them?"

"New guy. Owen's adopted him. Their lockers are next to each other."

"Poor guy. He doesn't look too nerdy. He's kind of cute, in fact."

"Justine! He's a total nerd. He's in one of my classes."

Justine sighed again. "Maybe all guys are looking good to me now that I know I'm going to be stuck with five hundred girls in red uniforms."

She got up. "Oh, well. I should get back home. I promised I'd baby-sit Alex while Christine gets her nails done. Alex is lucky—she doesn't have to wear uniform diapers."

I watched her go. She certainly looked very sad as she walked away. At least I liked my school and I still had friends here, even if I also had Lacey. Maybe I was luckier than Justine, Karen, and Roni. But I didn't feel lucky.

The sun moved onto the steps and I began to feel hot and uncomfortable. I was just trying to decide where to move to when Lacey came flying across the quad toward me.

"Ginger, guess what!" she yelled. "I made it. I'm on the squad. I'm a cheerleader!"

She did a little jump at the bottom of the steps, a jump I could never have managed.

"I'm so happy I could die!" squealed my country hick cousin.

Chapter

11

All the way home Lacey talked nonstop and loudly. "I can't believe it, Ginger. It's like a story in the movies, isn't it? Poor country girl goes to big city school and instantly becomes a star!"

"It's only cheerleading, Lacey," I growled. "Hardly stardom."

But she babbled on. "I can't tell you how much I was dreading going to school this morning and how scared I was. But now I've met all these nice people and the football players know me and I'm going to be a real honest-to-goodness cheerleader. Isn't that wonderful?"

I tried to tell myself that it *was* wonderful. At least Lacey would be out of my hair. She'd have her cheerleading friends and I wouldn't be responsible for her anymore. But a nagging little voice in my head whispered that it wasn't fair. Lacey had been at Alta Mesa for five minutes and was an instant success. Now she was going to walk around in her cute little uniform on rally and game days and everyone would know her.

I'd been here for a year and I was still just plain, ordinary me. Don't get me wrong—a cheerleader was the last thing on earth I wanted to be . . . well, one of the last things. Toilet bowl cleaner would come below it, and so would reptile house attendant *and* chicken feeder! But there was no way I wanted those snobby airheads as my friends. And jumping up and down with pom-poms yelling "Go, team!" seemed like a total waste of energy to me. But I would have liked some of the glamour and status that went along with the job. And now Lacey was going to have that.

I called Roni to ask how her day had been, but she wasn't home. I figured she might not want to talk about it anyway. If I told her about my classes and about sitting next to Josh White, she might think I was boasting. I thought about Josh White again. Was he just being friendly when he talked and joked with me this morning, or could it be more than that? I really liked the way his eyes twinkled when he smiled.

I found that I was smiling too as I headed to the kitchen for a snack. Todd was just coming in from the garage.

"Oh, by the way," he said. "Lacey wanted me to tell you that she won't be taking the bus with you in the morning. She's getting a ride in early with me so she can go through the routines with some of the cheerleaders."

"Oh," I said.

"Aren't you going to thank me?" he suggested with a grin. "I've just spared you the ordeal of having Lacey with you all the way to school."

"Oh, yeah, thanks," I muttered. Obviously he hadn't realized what I had—that Ben also rode into school with him in the mornings. I had seen Lacey's dreamy expression today as she arm wrestled Ben, and I'd say she was out to get him in the biggest way. Not that he'd ever be interested in my cousin the cowgirl, I reminded myself. But it took me a while to fall asleep that night.

Next morning Roni's yellow school bus roared past me as I stood alone at the stop. I didn't see her familiar black curls or big grin. *I hope she didn't run away from home over this*, I thought with a smile.

Roni had probably already found the best-looking guy at Oak Creek to drive her to school. She was too crazy not to be popular at such a small place. It wouldn't be as bad as she'd expected, I felt sure.

The city bus screeched to a halt in front of me. As I climbed on, I saw someone running up the street, waving and yelling.

"Hold on," I said to the driver. "I think there's someone else coming."

"She better be quick, then," the driver growled. "I'm behind schedule already."

"Hurry—" I yelled, then the words died in my throat. I could feel my mouth drop open in shock. "Roni?" I gasped. "What are you doing here?"

Roni swung herself on board and dropped her money into the box. "Hi," she said with a big smile. "Aren't you going to greet your best friend and ride partner?"

"What are you talking about? Why weren't you on the bus to Oak Creek?"

"Because I quit," she said.

"You quit? Are you serious?"

She went on grinning. "I tried to talk my parents out of it, but they wouldn't listen. So I went to school yesterday and I picked up my schedule and guess what? Instead of science and French and college-prep English, they'd put me in home ec and typing and reading for pleasure. So I went straight to the principal's office and said that there must be some mistake."

"And what did he say?"

"He said 'Sorry, little lady, but that was the only schedule we could pull together for you.' Then he even suggested that home ec and typing would be real useful to me later on, when I was looking for a job and running a home."

"I don't believe it!" I gasped. "I thought that attitude went out with the Dark Ages."

"So did I," Roni said.

"So what did you say?"

She grinned. "You know me," she said. "I've never been exactly shy when it comes to speaking my mind. I told him he'd promised my parents that he'd get me into good college-prep classes. And he just shrugged and said it wasn't his fault if he hadn't gotten the teachers to offer the courses."

"So what did you do?"

"I walked out," Roni said proudly. "I went straight home and told my mother I wasn't going back there again. She called my dad and he came home and when I'd finished telling them, they actually agreed with me. My mom said she didn't want her job to ruin my chances in life, so she'd look for something else. Then my dad called Alta Mesa and asked if it was too late for me to come back. And they said of course not, come on over and sign her up. So we did."

"Roni, I am so happy to see you," I said. "I can't tell you how depressed I was. It just wasn't the same without you."

"You're not half as happy as I am," she said. "Joe Garcia flicked rubber bands at the back of my neck all the way to school yesterday." She looked around. "So where's your cousin? Did you ditch her already?"

I made a face. "She ditched me," I said. "We created a monster, Roni. We were the ones who helped her look cute and told her how to act. So guess what she did, first day out? She went up onstage and arm wrestled the football players and got invited to join the cheerleading squad."

"No kidding? Lacey's a cheerleader? She's welcome to it. What did Chrissy Peterson say about her?"

"Chrissy Peterson was the one who invited her," I said.

"Well, now Lacey won't be following you around. That's good, right?"

"Yeah, except that she spent yesterday making eyes at my boyfriend and she rode to school with him this morning."

"No! Well, I wouldn't worry too much. Ben would never look twice at Lacey," Roni said firmly. "You guys are made for each other. Ben would never look at another girl."

"I hope that's true," I said. "Everyone around school is behaving like Ben is Mr. Stud now. I kept hearing how great he looked on the football field yesterday. And I'm just another boring sophomore."

"Oh, come on, think positive," Roni said. "I can't wait to get back! I'm going to try out for the play and maybe join the debate team, and I'll be the coolest— whoa! Sorry, ma'am." The bus took a corner too fast and Roni's backpack shot off her lap and caught a standing passenger in the back of the legs. The woman glared and examined her panty hose for possible snags. I grinned.

"It's great to have you back, Roni," I said. "Nothing's ever boring when you're around."

We got off the bus and headed for the school gate. "Did they announce anything about the fall play yet?" she asked. "Did you see any notices for auditions?"

"No, but then, I wasn't really looking," I said.

"The only thing I did hear was that there's going to be a new election for sophomore class president."

"Why?"

"Don moved away."

"Good. I thought he was too dorky for president anyway. Speaking of dorks, how is Owen?"

"Looking quite sharp, but still the same old Owen we know and love," I said, laughing. "I nearly had to sit next to him yesterday. Oh, and he's got another new nerd in the pack now. Justine stopped by yesterday and she thought he was cute."

"Justine is suffering from pre-travel stress," Roni said. "What do you have first period?"

"World history with Levitan."

"Me too. Let's go."

"I already have a seat," I said as I dumped my books on the seat behind Josh. "If I'd known you were coming, I'd have saved you one."

"That's okay. I like it at the back better," Roni said.

"I thought your friend had transferred to another school," Josh said, turning around to talk to me.

"That was yesterday," I said. "Today it's Alta Mesa. She's trying out a different school every day. That way you don't get bored."

He laughed. "Sounds good to me," he said. "You know, Ginger, I was thinking . . ."

"About what?"

"About class president. Have you ever thought of running?"

"Me?"

"Sure, why not?" he said. "You'd be great."

"I'd be terrible, Josh. I'm a nobody. I wouldn't know what to do."

"Sure you would! You're not a nobody. Everyone was impressed when you were on TV last year when you saved that mountain from the developers. I saw you on the news, and I thought you handled yourself really well. I'd say you were a natural."

"I don't know," I said, laughing nervously. "I never saw myself as presidential material."

"Think about it," Josh said. "I'll help you with your campaign if you decide to run."

I sat in a daze all through world history. President? Me? And Josh wanted to help me with my campaign. A picture swam into my head—Josh and I, sitting with our heads close together, late at night, as we wrote my speech. "This is good stuff, Ginger," he'd say. "After you win, we'll be together on class council all year. . . ."

Wait a minute! Was that what I really wanted? Was it really time to ditch Ben and find myself a new guy? If he didn't ditch me first, I thought, remembering Lacey. Maybe Ben *was* going to ditch me for Lacey. Well, I'd show him that I didn't care.

But I did care. That was the problem. I really didn't want to lose Ben. I couldn't even imagine life without him. But having Josh as my campaign manager might not be such a bad idea—it would make Ben sit up and take notice that quiet little Ginger wasn't such a nobody anymore.

At the end of world history Roni and I walked across campus together.

"It's as if I've just woken up from a nightmare," Roni said. "I can't tell you how good it feels to be in a class of fun, normal, smart people, not in a place where the main conversation consists of 'Woo-ee, how about them Cardinals, huh?'"

I nodded in understanding. "We seem to have all the smart kids in that world history class," I commented.

"Do you think it was a mistake?"

"What?"

"That you and I got assigned to it?"

"Speak for yourself," I said. "I'm sure that I belong there. Anyone who saved Spirit Rock has a good feel for history in the making."

"Ha!" she said, giving me a friendly nudge. "Just because you sit behind Josh White, you're getting a swelled head." She paused, then went on, "Now that's a guy I'd like to know better. He's smart without being a geek, if you know what I mean. And he's funny too. Even Mr. Levitan had to laugh today when he made that remark about Alexander the Great."

I could feel my cheeks getting hotter. I was suddenly uncomfortable talking about Josh with Roni. Not that there was anything to hide . . . well, except the president thing. I just wasn't ready to talk about that yet.

"It's great that you're sitting so close to Josh," Roni said. "When you get to know him better, you can introduce me."

"He already knows who you are."

"Are you serious?"

"Yeah, he asked where you were yesterday."

"He asked about me? All right! This is going to be my lucky year, I can tell. Everything's coming up Roni's."

"Don't you dare sing in the middle of the quad," I hissed, grabbing her arm.

"Speaking of singing, I've got to check out the play," Roni said. "I hope it's funny. I hope I get a big part. Oh, Ginger. This is all so great." She was dancing around like a little kid, and I was excited for her.

I'd be feeling the same way if I'd been rescued from Oak Creek by a miracle.

We had different classes for the rest of the morning, so we didn't meet up again until lunchtime. Lacey and I came out of the locker room after a boring hour of physical conditioning.

"I'm meeting Roni by our tree," I said to her. "You want to join us?"

"Gee, thanks, Cuz," Lacey said, "but I promised Chrissy and the girls that I'd eat with them. I hope you don't mind."

"I'm sure we'll survive without you, Lacey."

She squeezed my arm. "I'll try and make time to eat with you real soon, Cuz."

I watched her skip off toward the cafeteria. Then I walked over to our tree, where Roni was already diving into her lunch bag. "I'm starving," she said. "Isn't your cousin coming?"

"Lacey was last seen running in the direction of Chrissy Peterson and the cheerleaders," I said. "But she was sweet about it. She promised me she'd make time to do lunch with me real soon."

Roni grinned. "You're right. We have created a monster. She'll start giving you air kisses soon."

"At least we have a peaceful lunch with just the two of us," I said. "It seems weird, doesn't it?"

Roni nodded. "No Karen and no Justine. I really miss them, especially Karen. She called me last night, you know."

"She did?" I asked, slightly annoyed that Karen hadn't called me. I knew Karen and Roni were close because they both had to suffer with parents who were raised in traditional backgrounds. But it still bugged me that Karen hadn't called me too. "How's she doing?" I asked.

"Okay, I guess," Roni said. "She didn't say she wasn't liking it, but she wasn't bubbling over with enthusiasm either. She said the other students were really dedicated. All they talked about in the cafeteria was music."

"I guess you have to be like that if you're going to study something seriously," I said. "Maybe we're lucky that we're not super talented in anything."

"Speak for yourself," Roni said. "I happen to be one of the world's great actors."

I snorted.

"Hey!" she said. "Some friend you are. You're supposed to be on my side. Oh, and speaking of being on my side . . ." She glanced around furtively. "I'm glad it's just the two of us, because we can start making serious plans."

"About what?"

"I've made a big decision," Roni said grandly. "There's an election coming up for class pres, right? And Josh is on class council, right? And he's very cute, right?"

"Right," I said cautiously.

"So I've decided to run for president, and you can be my campaign manager!"

Chapter

12

"Caught you by surprise, didn't I?" Roni said, laughing at my shocked expression. "What? You don't think I can win? You think I'd be making a fool of myself?"

"No," I managed to say. "I think you've got as good a chance as anybody . . . it's just that . . . what if I wanted to run?"

A big grin spread across Roni's face. "You? Get serious, Ginger. Why would you want to run for president? You hate having to get up in front of people. You're not loud like me. Everyone knows who I am. Besides, you don't need an excuse to be near Josh. You've already got the world's nicest boyfriend."

I didn't say anything. She stopped smiling. "You

weren't seriously thinking about running, were you?"

"I might have been," I said. "J—um, somebody suggested to me that I ought to run, and I was thinking about it."

Roni put an arm around my shoulders. "Come on, Ginger, old pal, best buddy in the world, give me a break here. I'm the one who wants to get close to Josh. Not that that's a good reason to run for office, but I have to admit the thought of all those cozy class council meetings is very tempting. And we'd have a blast if you were my campaign manager. You know we work well together. What do you say? You will let me run, won't you? Please?"

"I'll think about it," I said.

And I did think about it, all the rest of the day. Roni was right about a couple of things. I didn't really enjoy getting up in front of people and hamming it up. And she was great at that sort of thing. Plus, everyone knew her from the school play. That was another point in her favor. People knew me too, from the time they saw me on TV and from track team, but Roni had been a star in the play. Realistically, she probably had a better chance of winning the election than I did.

And she was interested in Josh and she didn't have a boyfriend right now. It made sense for her to run and me to be the campaign manager. But it bugged me that she always took it for granted that *she'd* be the star and *I'd* be the sidekick. Just once in my life, I wanted to be the one who mattered.

I was still thinking about it that evening as I did my homework. I was no nearer to making up my mind when the phone rang. I just hoped it wasn't Roni wanting an answer.

"Ginger, it's Lacey for you," Todd yelled down the hall.

"Is she calling to apologize because she won't be able to ride the bus with me, due to an unexpected breakfast meeting with the cheerleaders?" I asked as I pushed past him to get the phone. "I bet she expects me to be heartbroken about it . . . or is it brokenhearted?"

"Don't ask me," Todd said. "I've never been either."

I picked up the phone.

"Hi, Ginger, it's me," Lacey said. "Sorry to bother you, but I wondered if you could give me Ben's address."

"Ben's address?" I think it came out as a squeak.

"That's right," she bubbled on. "I meant to ask him for it this morning and I clean forgot. I know he lives around here and I just wanted to pop over there."

149

"You want to go over to Ben's house tonight?" I demanded. A red bubble of anger was growing inside my head.

"Sure. I've got something I just have to show him. Something we were talking about earlier today, and I know he'll want to see."

"Something that's so important it can't wait until you're at school tomorrow?" I demanded. I felt like I was about to explode. "What did you do, find gold in your backyard? Or did Jerry Rice stop by your place and promise to give him a few pointers on playing wide receiver?"

"Nothing like that, silly," she said, giggling loudly. "It's just, um, something we were discussing this morning and I told him I'd look into it and now I have. That's all. Do you have a problem with that?"

"I sure do," I said. "Do you think it isn't totally obvious what you're up to, Lacey?"

"I don't understand, Cuz."

She had bugged me when she called me Cousin Ginger, but this new Cuz thing was even worse. "Oh, come on, Lacey. I'm not stupid, you know. I've seen the way you've been going after Ben. I saw you looking at him at school. And now you just want to drop by his house at eight o'clock at night?"

She laughed, that annoying donkey laugh of hers.

"Oh, shoot, Cousin Ginger. You didn't think that I was making a play for your guy, did you?"

"I can't think of any other good reason you'd want to show up at a strange guy's house after dark," I said.

"You've got it all wrong, Ginger," Lacey said. She wasn't laughing now. "This is just something I promised I'd show Ben and I know he'd want to see it right away."

"Like what?"

"Oh . . . nothing big, just . . . uh, something we were looking into together. But you really don't have to worry, Cuz. I promise you that I'm not after your boyfriend. Cross my heart and hope to die."

I didn't really believe her, but I gave her Ben's address. I couldn't *not* give it to her, or it would seem as if I didn't trust her—or him. Plus, Dad would kill me if I was mean to Lacey. But I tossed and turned all night, worrying. And I remembered that Ben hadn't even called me since school started.

The next morning on the bus Roni was bubbling with her normal energy.

"I've been thinking of all these great campaign ideas," she said. "How about if I bake cookies and write my name across them in frosting? Isn't that cute? And I'd like to get the school radio station going again . . . and maybe even branch out to our own TV channel. I can see myself as an anchor-woman."

"You think you'll have time to fit in any classes between being president and anchor and having the lead in all the plays?" I knew I was being grouchy, but I was annoyed. I had to admit that her ideas were good. She would probably be a much better president than me.

Roni looked at me questioningly. "Do you really want to run for pres yourself?" she asked. "Because if it really means that much to you . . . well, I do have plays and things."

"No, it's okay. You do it," I said. "You'll obviously be way better at it than me."

"Are you really sure?"

"It's yours," I snapped. "I am stepping down, bowing out, withdrawing from the race. There. Are you satisfied?"

She looked at me doubtfully for a minute, then she grinned. "Okay, if you insist, I'll announce my candidacy today. Maybe we can work on my campaign tonight?"

I sort of grunted, which was the nearest I was going to come to saying yes.

Roni was silent for a moment. Then she said, "You

know, you may be right. I hope I have enough time to be class president *and* be in the play. If I'm really going to be a professional actor some day, I need all the experience I can get. But public speaking as president will be useful too, I guess. I'll have to find Drew. I bet he can give me pointers."

"I bet he can," I couldn't resist teasing. Drew had been sophomore class president last year. He'd also been Roni's boyfriend last year. I don't think she'll get over him as long as she lives.

Roni grinned. "I wasn't thinking what you were thinking," she said. "Drew and I have agreed to be friends, and I want to keep it like that. Right now my thoughts are more on Josh White. Does he have a girlfriend?"

"How would I know?" I asked, hoping my face wouldn't give me away. I was very tempted to say that I thought he liked a girl in our class, but I didn't. After all, I did have Ben. I couldn't be greedy, could I?

Roni leaped off the bus, still supercharged with energy. "Okay, this is the plan," she said. "First we check out tryouts for the play. Then I'll swing by the adviser's office and sign up for president."

"Then you sign up for the debate team, future farmers of America, young homemakers, and girls' volleyball—all before our first class," I quipped.

She grinned again. "I'll leave the future farmers to you," she said. "After all your chicken experience, you're a shoo-in for president of that!"

I couldn't believe it! My own best friend insulting me! It seemed like she was saying I could be president of future farmers, but not of something big and important like the sophomore class. I glared at her back all the way to the notice boards.

There was a big poster about play auditions, which were that afternoon. "*End of the Line*," Roni read. "I've never heard of that play, have you?"

I shook my head. "It says it's a modern Russian drama," I said. "Doesn't sound like your thing at all."

"I can be modern and Russian if I want to, dahlink," Roni said, putting on a deep voice with a phony Russian accent. "We great actors can do anything, you know. Will you come with me to tryouts tonight?"

"You don't need me," I said. "You're an old pro at this."

"Sure I need you," Roni said. "You know I'm always terrified at auditions. And I hate riding the bus home alone."

"I should be a paid bus escort," I growled. "First Lacey and now you. Am I the only person who can do anything alone in this school?"

"You're my best friend and an all-around wonderful person," Roni said, giving me a quick hug as she hurried to her locker.

"So what do you think?" Josh asked me as I slid into my seat for world history.

"About what?"

"Running for pres. Did you think it over?"

"Yeah, and I've decided against it," I said. "I'm just not the type, Josh. I clam up in front of an audience. Someone like Roni would be better than me."

"Don't put yourself down," Josh said. "I think you'd be great. And I'd really like it if you were on our class council. The other people are so boring. At least we could have fun together."

It sounded wonderful.

"You don't have to sign up until tomorrow," Josh said. "Think it over some more, okay? I've got some great campaign ideas. I bet I could guarantee a win for you."

"Doing what? Paying people to vote?" I laughed.

"Don't knock it. It works. How do you think people get elected in Washington?"

You are such fun, Josh White, I thought as I watched the back of his dark, curly head. *It would be such fun planning a campaign with you.* But Roni had been my best friend all my life and she'd set her heart on this. I couldn't let her down.

After school I let Roni talk me into going to auditions with her.

"There's hardly anyone here," she muttered as we went into the auditorium. "Nothing like the spring musical. A good part should be a cinch. I wonder who the female lead is?"

She must have been talking loudly because a tall, earnest-looking senior came over to her. "You're Roni. I saw you in the musical," he said. "I'm Derek. I'm directing this as my senior project. It's a very intense, dramatic play. It's about people who are released from a prison camp in Siberia and they're on a train going home, but of course with all the upheavals in Russia, they've got no home to go to."

"Sounds like a million laughs," Roni whispered to me.

"The heroine, Natasha, jumps from the train and kills herself," Derek added.

"Are you sure you want to do this?" I muttered to Roni as he walked away. "It sounds so depressing."

"I need a chance to play drama," Roni said. I could see that in her mind she was already Natasha, about to leap from the train. I sighed and slid into a seat to one side where I could get on with my homework. Derek called people onstage and assigned parts for a read-through. Roni was given Natasha. She looked at me and gave me a thumbs-up sign.

They started to read. One thing soon became very clear. As well as being dramatic and depressing, the play was written in very difficult language. Roni stumbled a couple of times. Then she threw out her arms and exclaimed, "It was a great catastrophe!" Only she pronounced it "cat-a-strofe."

Everyone burst out laughing.

"That's pronounced cat-*as*-trophy," Derek said.

Roni's face was bright red. "I know that," she said. "I was just too much into the part."

Obviously it totally threw her, because after that she started pronouncing more and more things wrong. And the worst thing was that each time, everyone laughed. Soon people were laughing at all of her lines.

When she pronounced "hyperbole" as "hyperbowl," someone from the audience yelled, "Is that like the Super Bowl?" and the whole audition fell to pieces.

Derek stormed up onstage. "This is a serious play, people," he said. "It is a play of great suffering and you're turning it into one-liners." He glared at Roni.

"I didn't mean to," she said.

"I don't think this is going to work," Derek told her. "Everyone knows you for your comedy. We'd find it hard to get the right mood with you onstage. I couldn't risk the audience laughing in the wrong places."

"So you're saying you don't want me?" Roni demanded. Her face was flushed and her eyes were sparking black fire.

"I don't think I can take that risk," he said. "Maybe you should just stick to comedy. You've obviously got a flair for it."

"Fine," Roni said. "This play was too boring anyway. Who wants to see a train going through Russia?" She stalked off the stage. "Come on, Ginger, we're going home," she said.

The moment we were outside she exploded. "How dare he? Is he stupid or what? He fires the only person who can really act! Now he's left with a bunch of dreary nothings, no personality, no looks, just completely blah! It'll serve him right when his play is a total failure!"

"Come on, Roni," I said. "You sound like a prima donna. I mean, you did wreck his audition. You made some real bloopers up there."

She glared at me. "Some friend you are," she yelled. "You're supposed to be on my side, not against me. I saw you laughing with the rest of them."

"Chill out, Roni," I said quietly, because she was really screaming now. "Of course I'm not against you. Why are you getting so upset about this? Just face it—serious drama is not your thing."

"How would you know?" she demanded. "Just because you're not talented and you don't have the personality to be a star . . ."

Boy, was she pushing the wrong buttons. "You really have nerve," I said, "after I've fallen over backward to be nice to you. If that's the way you feel, forget about having me for a campaign manager. You'll find out who's got personality when you have to run against me."

"You're going to run against *me* for president?" She snorted. "You really think you stand a chance?"

"We'll see," I said. "I can tell you one person who thinks I'll make a great class president."

"Who is it—one of the nerds? Or someone who needs new glasses?"

"Neither," I said smoothly. "It's Josh White. He's the one who wants me to run, and he's volunteered to be my campaign manager."

I swept past her to the bus stop and sat as far away as possible from her all the way home.

Chapter

13

I took an early bus to school the next morning so that I didn't have to see Roni, and I got to class early so that I could catch Josh the moment he came into the room.

"I've changed my mind," I said as he sat down. "I've decided to run for president after all."

His face lit up. "All right! You're going to be great. I run a mean campaign. We have to get together and plan strategy."

"Sure. Anytime you're free." I gave him my brightest smile.

I was very conscious of Roni, sitting at the back of the classroom, pretending to be looking for something in her backpack.

At the end of world history she hurried to catch

up with me. "Ginger, you're not really serious about running, are you?"

"As serious as you are."

She attempted a smile. "Come on, Ginger. This won't work. People will think it's really weird if we run against each other."

"Then withdraw. There's still time."

"Ginger, we're best buddies," Roni said. "We've always done stuff together."

I looked at her coldly. "I'm sure you'll be delighted to get rid of a best buddy who has no talent and no personality."

"Ginger, you know I was just kidding. . . ."

"And I know you want to get Josh, too. Sorry, Charlie. He's already shown who he's interested in."

"What about Ben?" she demanded. "What's he going to think when you're spending evenings with your campaign manager?"

"Ben hasn't even called me since school started," I said. "But he's had time to invite Lacey over to show him something at eight o'clock at night. I think he's another person who needs to learn that Ginger Hartman is not a doormat or a slave."

"Are you saying that I treat you like a slave?"

"Let's just say a faithful sidekick. Remember, I'm the one with no personality."

"You said it."

I glared at her. "You're in for a big shock! When I'm the sophomore class president, I'll have to sit on class council with Josh and go to student council meetings with Drew." I gave her a smile.

"Dream on," Roni snapped. "You haven't got a prayer. All I have to do is turn on my dazzling smile, my great speaking ability—"

"Your mispronounced words?"

"I hate you!"

"I hate you too!"

"Roni! Ginger! Wait up, it's me!" The voice echoed the whole length of the social studies hallway. We both spun around.

"Karen!" we yelled at the same time.

Karen came flying toward us, grinning from ear to ear. "Surprise, huh?" she cried, throwing her arms around us.

"They let you out of violin practice to visit us?" Roni asked.

Karen shook her head. "I quit," she said happily.

"Karen, you didn't!" I exclaimed. "You quit the conservatory?"

She nodded. "I knew from the first second that I didn't belong there," she said. "I felt like a total phony. The other kids loved their music. They couldn't wait until they joined an orchestra someday. And I . . . I don't even like the violin that much. Every practice session was a chore for me."

"What did your folks say?" Roni asked. "They were so thrilled about this conservatory scholarship."

Karen grimaced. "They weren't happy. You know they always dreamed of me being a professional musician. But I hated it at the conservatory. I don't mind playing the violin, but there are other things I like even better—like my friends, and the newspaper, and even my classes here. I just want to be a normal teenager, not some nerd who can only play the violin. I don't want to end up a geek like that guy I told you about at music camp."

"So you're coming back here?" I asked.

"I just finished enrolling and planning my schedule. It's incredible! I get to be with my friends again. The three of us can do everything together. So what's new? What have I missed so far?"

Roni and I looked at each other.

"Not much," I said.

"So are we meeting at the same place for lunch?"

"I might be kind of busy," Roni said at the same time that I said, "I have to go to the office to sign some papers."

Karen looked from Roni's face to mine. "What's up?" she asked.

"Ginger is running against me for class president," Roni said.

"Actually Roni's running against me," I said.

"I declared my candidacy first."

"But I had been asked to run the day before. I just didn't go around blabbing it to everybody."

Karen looked horrified. "You guys! You're best friends. Be nice to each other. Running for office shouldn't spoil a friendship."

"You're right," Roni said. "When I'm elected, I'll be very kind and sympathetic to Ginger, who has just lost."

"Huh! I'll throw you a petal from my corsage when I go to the next formal with Josh."

"Guys!" Karen yelled. "I was so excited to come back here and now I've stepped into the middle of a war! I guess eating lunch together is a bad idea. You two should stay away from each other until you can make up."

"Sorry, Karen," I said. "I didn't mean to include you in this. I'm sure we're both really glad to see you back. Maybe Roni will wise up soon."

"Maybe Ginger will."

"Well, you both better snap out of it," Karen said,

"because here come the nerds."

"They've improved this year," Roni said.

"And they've got a new nerd in the pack," I added. "Justine thought he was cute, but I think he fits right in with them."

"A new nerd? Where?"

"He's there. You can't see him because he's behind Wolfgang. I think that's his briefcase sticking out. There he is now, see?"

"Ahhhhh!" Karen darted behind Roni and me. "Hide me," she whispered.

"What's wrong?"

"It's him! It's Jeremy! The nerd from my music camp who made my life miserable."

"You're kidding."

"No, it's definitely him. I'd know those glasses anywhere."

"They're heading this way," Roni announced.

"What are we going to do?" I asked. There was no place to hide. We were trapped in the middle of the hallway.

"Just don't move," Karen hissed. "Stand very close together. Maybe they'll just walk past."

The nerd pack approached.

"Hi, girls," Owen cooed. "Enjoying school so far?"

"Until now," Roni said dryly.

"I see you're running for president, Roni," Owen said.

"That's right."

"And I am too," I said. Roni glared at me.

"Wonderful. I think close races are exciting," Owen said. "Democracy at its best. Magnificent. It's what this country was built on."

Karen's nerd stood behind Owen, studying his shoelaces. Wolfgang and Walter were grinning at us hopefully. Ronald, now taller than ever, was looking at us with a frown.

"Do you have a problem, Karen?" he asked. "Why are you hiding behind Roni and Ginger?"

I was tempted to say that Karen wasn't really there, that she was only a hologram. Knowing the nerds, they'd probably buy that theory. But I didn't have time.

"Ronald, you don't ask a girl questions like that," Roni scolded.

Ronald blushed bright pink. "I just thought maybe she had a button missing from her shirt or her zipper broke or something. I know annoying things like that are always happening to me."

This interesting conversation didn't get any further because the new nerd had pushed past Wolfgang. "Karen? Is that you?" he demanded, his face totally alight. "It is you! It is you!"

"Jeremy, what are you doing here?" Karen snapped. Roni and I stared at her in surprise. Karen never yelled at people.

"My family moved to Phoenix," Jeremy said, "and I remembered you'd told me the name of your school. So I persuaded my parents to let me come here. But someone said you weren't here anymore. I've been looking for you all week."

If I'd been Karen, I'd have told him that I was just visiting, but she's too honest. "I wasn't here," she said. "I started out at the music conservatory, but I quit."

"You went to the music conservatory?" Jeremy yelled. "And you quit? Why?"

"I didn't like it."

"You didn't like it? How could you not like it? It's like heaven and utopia all rolled into one."

"It wasn't for me."

"I can't believe it," Jeremy said. "I'd give my right arm to go to the music conservatory. Or, at least, I don't think I could give my right arm, because then I wouldn't be able to play the violin. . . ."

Roni started to laugh, then I did too. I couldn't help myself. Jeremy was so serious and intense. At least the laughter broke the tension.

"I've got a great idea, Jeremy," Karen said. "Why don't you apply for my place? It's open now that I quit."

"Your place?" I could see he was going through torment. "But you're here now. Why would I want to be somewhere you're not?"

"Better music training?"

"Music or love, what a terrible decision," Jeremy said. "I'll have to think about it."

The nerd pack moved off. Karen stared after them with a look of dismay on her face. "Now do you see what I mean? Is the guy nuts or what? 'Music or love'— normal people don't say things like that, do they?"

"Maybe he's destined to become the next Beethoven and they'll make a movie about his love for you," Roni quipped.

"It might just include a dramatic scene of me throwing myself off a cliff if he stays here," Karen said. "Right now that dumb conservatory doesn't seem so bad."

"Don't leave us again, Karen," Roni said. "We missed you. We want you here."

"Don't worry. I'm not seriously considering going back there. But you guys have got to help me," Karen said. "I don't care if you're not speaking to each other. You've got to team up to protect me from Jeremy!"

Chapter

14

The first football game was on Friday night. It was just a scrimmage, so it didn't really count, but I found that I was pretty excited about it. It would be the first time I'd see Ben playing as a senior—the first time I'd be the girlfriend of the star wide receiver. I knew that shouldn't mean anything to me, but it did. Maybe I was itching to get some attention, even if it was only rubbed-off fame.

Last year, Ben had spent most of his time on the bench, looking frustrated. It wasn't until almost the end of the season that the coach gave him a chance. He'd proved himself by scoring the winning touchdown. It was amazing when I thought of it. The Ben I grew up with was quiet and shy—with other people, I mean. He was never shy with me. I had always been his little buddy, the one he threw the football with or squirted with the hose on hot days. I didn't like to think about that now, because it made me feel panicky at the thought of losing him.

We had realized, of course, that we were taking a chance when we changed from being just friends. We knew that one day we could fall out of love, and that it could wreck our friendship too. But having Ben as my first boyfriend was everything I'd dreamed of. I just hadn't expected him to blossom into a popular football hero.

I hoped this football game would be all I dreamed of, too. I imagined myself sitting on one of those front bleachers, yelling encouragement to him when he did something spectacular. After the game he'd put his arm around me as we headed for the locker rooms. Maybe then I'd realize that I'd been worrying for nothing. He hadn't been losing interest in me after all.

The game was kind of boring. We were way better than the other team and the coach took his starters out after the first quarter. It was lonely without Roni sitting beside me. And out of the corner of my eye I saw Lacey in her new uniform being loud and airheaded with the other cheerleaders.

As soon as the game was over, I came down from the bleachers to where Ben was sitting with the other starters. "Good game," I said.

"No, it wasn't," he said. "We played badly. Luckily they were so bad that it didn't matter, but any good team would have walked all over us."

"It looked okay to me," I said. "You made a great catch."

"Sure. One," he said, glancing at his teammates.

"So are we going somewhere to celebrate?" I asked.

He didn't meet my gaze. "Uh . . . sorry, Ginger, but we're having this team thing. Spaghetti dinner over at Tony's house. The coach wants us to work on team bonding and unity, and he's also going to show us the video he took of the game."

"That's going to be painful," one of his teammates joked. "Especially when he shows me dropping the ball over and over in slow motion."

"You can get home okay, can't you?" Ben asked, putting a hand on my arm. "Do you want me to find you a ride?"

"That's okay. I can find my own ride," I said.

He must have picked up the tone in my voice. "I'm sorry about this, Ginger," he said. "You know what coaches are like. We'll do something over the weekend, maybe."

"Maybe," I echoed.

I walked away alone. As I passed the girls' locker room a group of cheerleaders was just going inside.

"Hey, Angie, did you get directions to Tony's house?" one of them yelled.

"Don't need them. Brad's taking us in his truck," Angie called back.

I stomped past, unseen. *Some football bonding,* I thought. Maybe Lacey would be there too. It was clear now that I didn't matter to Ben at all. Nothing mattered but cheerleaders.

Okay, Ben Campbell, I thought furiously. *You've made it very clear. Well, see if I care. I'm running for president and if Josh happens to be interested in me, then I'm not going to stop him!*

I wished I'd gotten Josh's address so I could have invited him over to work on my campaign. We could've spent the whole weekend working together at my house. And Ben could have stumbled across us having a great time.

I looked through the phone book, but there were a couple of pages of Whites and I had no idea where he lived. So I gave up and thought about the campaign instead. Election day was only a week away. A whole week to work with Josh. I should be able to come up with a killer speech by then, and there were plenty of evenings for us to get together. I circled the big day with bright yellow marker on my calendar.

And then I noticed another day circled. I was shocked to realize that it was also only a week until my birthday. With all the upheaval I'd completely forgotten about it. Until now it had always been Roni who made sure I celebrated my birthday. I guess men aren't very good about parties and things. At least my dad isn't. His idea of a great birthday is to say, "Here's fifty dollars. Go out and buy yourself something and take your friends for ice cream."

If it wasn't for Roni, I'd never have had a party. I felt tears stinging at the back of my eyes. This year I wouldn't have Roni around. This year I'd have no party and probably no friends to celebrate with. How had we gotten into this crazy war in the first place? I couldn't even remember what had started it. But I couldn't see any way out of it, unless I took myself out of the race. And I wasn't about to do that.

Suddenly I remembered that I did have someone who owed me a giant favor—Lacey.

I called Lacey first thing Saturday morning. "I need help making posters this weekend," I said.

"I don't know, Ginger," she said. "I'm kind of busy this weekend. I promised, um, certain people that I'd meet them to do . . . certain things. . . ."

"Lacey! I spent all that time helping you on the farm and then getting ready for school. I deserve a little help now."

"I'll try and make time," she said. "I guess I could fit you in before noon."

Great, I thought as I put down the phone. *This is the person who was so shy that she thought she'd never survive at my school and now she has trouble fitting me in?* Well, she would just have to make time, because I intended to find out exactly what happened at that spaghetti dinner.

I went out and bought poster board and big markers and sparkly stickers for my posters. Lacey showed up around eleven.

"I'm not the greatest artist," she said.

"I need slogans," I said.

"I'm not the greatest creative writer."

I glared at her. "Can you stick on neon stars?"

"Oh, sure. I can do that," she said. "Little glitter stars. How cute!"

We did some VOTE FOR GINGER, which were very boring. Then we tried GINGER, SHE'S THE ONE—not much better. *If only Josh was here,* I thought. *I bet he'd have a million great ideas.* Neither Lacey nor I could draw a person who looked like me, so we couldn't do anything really creative. But I did manage a megaphone, and I wrote under it, *Ginger, she'll make your voice heard.*

"That's good," Lacey agreed, so we did several of those. Lacey stuck glitter all over the megaphones.

"So, Lacey," I said casually, when she was totally absorbed in not spilling the glitter. "How was the party last night?"

"What party?"

"The spaghetti feed over at Tony's."

"I didn't hear anything about a spaghetti feed," she said. "I went straight home."

I had to believe her, because I knew she blushed bright red whenever she told a lie. So at least she hadn't spent yesterday evening with Ben. The only question then was, who had?

"Was it only the older cheerleaders who went?" I asked.

"To what?" she asked innocently. "Hey, look at the time! I gotta fly," she exclaimed, leaping up and scattering glitter everywhere. "Good luck with your posters, Cuz."

She was gone before I could ask her where she had to rush off to. I looked out the window to see her running down my street in the direction of Roni's house. *No way,* I told myself. *She'd never dare . . .* but she did. When she reached the end of the block,

I could almost swear I saw her turn into Roni's house. I couldn't believe it—my own cousin, turning traitor on me.

I went on working alone on my posters. I thought of calling Karen for help, but I knew that she'd feel awkward about helping me and not Roni. I even thought of calling Justine, but she was probably going crazy with last-minute packing. They were all set to fly out next Saturday. We were supposed to be going over to her house on Friday night. Even that would be awkward now with me and Roni not talking to each other.

When I heard the front door open I didn't even look up.

"Wow, some production line!" Ben's voice said behind me, making me jump. "I heard you were running for class president. Good for you, Ginger." He sat down opposite me at the table. "Need some help?"

"I'm almost done," I said without looking up.

"So . . . uh, did you get home okay last night?"

"No, I'm still out there wandering the streets," I snapped.

He laughed nervously. "I felt kind of bad about letting you go home alone, but you know what these team things are like."

"I can imagine," I said. "Did you have fun at Tony's house?"

"If you call it fun to have the coach freeze-frame you and show the whole team how you were totally out of position," he said.

"I'm sure Danielle and Angie managed to cheer you up," I commented. "That's what cheerleaders are for, isn't it?"

I did look up then, and his face was bright red. "Oh yeah, some of the cheerleaders did stop by, but the coach sent them home again. He said it was a working dinner."

"I see," I said.

"Look, Ginger, I'm sorry I'm so busy right now," he said. "The beginning of the football season is always bad. I just hope you understand that I don't have time to do stuff with you. The team has to come first—that's just the way it is. And the guys are getting together again tonight, I'm afraid. . . ."

"That's okay," I said. "Actually it works out fine. I'm really busy on this campaign right now. Josh White is going to be helping me. Do you know Josh? He's my campaign manager and he's a whiz at all this speech and poster stuff, since he's been on class councils all his life. He's really funny." I glanced at Ben. He looked even redder than before. "So we've got a very busy weekend ahead of us," I continued. "I wouldn't have had time for you anyway."

"Great," Ben said awkwardly. "I have some errands to run. You . . . uh, haven't seen Lacey, have you?"

"Lacey? You're looking for Lacey and you don't have time for me?"

"Yeah, well, we're doing this . . . this . . . *project* together. I promised her I'd take her where she had to go in my truck. Her mom said she was over here."

"Try Roni's house," I snapped. I began coloring furiously with my big black marker.

Ben touched my shoulder gently. "Ginger, don't be mad at me," he said. "It's nothing, really. Just a little dumb errand Lacey wants me to run for her."

"I'm not mad," I said. "I just have to get this done before Josh gets here."

I heard him let himself out, and I ran to the phone book. Somehow I was going to have to find Josh and get him over here. I'd teach Ben Campbell to have time for Lacey and not for me!

I started calling all the J. Whites, on the theory that boys are always named after their fathers. The first two said "Sorry, you have the wrong number," but the third guy yelled, "I'm sick of you kids!" so I was scared to go on.

I finished up the posters alone and tried not to

178

think of Ben and Lacey cruising around in his truck, or of Roni and Lacey working on her campaign together. I'd show them I didn't care if they all snuck around behind my back.

By the end of the weekend I had a whole stack of posters done. They weren't too professional, but at least I had a lot. I planned to get to school super early on Monday morning so that I could get all the best spots on the walls. I set my alarm for six and rode the early bus in. Roni wasn't at the bus stop. At least this was one advantage I'd have over her—my posters would be everywhere before she could even put up a single one!

When I turned into the hallway where my locker was, the first thing I saw was a huge, glittery poster.

VOTE FOR RONI, SHE'S THE ONE.

"Ahhhhh," I yelled to the empty hall. There were Roni posters everywhere. There was even a Roni poster reading, *She'll make your voice heard,* with a picture of a megaphone. How dare she! Lacey must have told her my ideas and she copied. *They're perfect together,* I thought, *a traitor and a copycat.* I wasn't sure who I was more angry at—Roni for being friends with a girl she knew I hated, or Lacey for stealing her own cousin's best friend! Lacey seemed to be stealing everyone I cared about.

I dumped my pile of posters on the ground with a sigh. "I guess I better get to work," I mumbled. Finding unused spots on the walls was hard—there weren't many, and they were all in the dark corners where nobody ever went. When I finished hanging my posters, I stood by our lockers and waited for Roni to arrive.

"You have some nerve," I yelled as soon as she set foot inside the door.

"What?"

"How did you manage to get your posters up before me?"

"I came by yesterday and sweet-talked the janitor," she said, grinning triumphantly. "You could have done the same thing."

"You stole my ideas!"

"I did not steal your ideas. I came up with them myself."

"Oh, sure. So how come your posters say exactly the same thing mine do? Huh?"

"Maybe you stole my ideas."

"Oh, right. You're the one who sent your little spy over to my house!"

"My what? What are you talking about?"

"Lacey. I did my posters first thing on Saturday morning, and Lacey helped me. And then she went running straight over to your house. I watched her do it! I can't believe you'd use my own cousin to spy on me!"

"That was something totally different," Roni said. "We didn't even mention posters."

"Oh, sure, I believe you."

"I don't care whether you believe me or not," she yelled. "You're being totally childish about this."

"At least I'm playing fair."

"I think you're a sore loser."

"I haven't lost, and I don't intend to."

We went to our side-by-side lockers, taking out books noisily and then slamming the doors. I guess it would have looked funny if it hadn't been so tragic.

"You made posters," Josh said as I walked into the world history classroom. "You should have called me. I have great poster ideas and my graphics program prints really well."

"I wanted to call you," I said, "but I didn't know your number. I started working my way through all the Whites in the phone book, but I gave up after a man yelled at me."

Josh grinned. "Sorry. That was dumb of me. Here, I'll write down my phone number for you. Call me tonight, okay?" I glanced up to make sure Roni was looking as he scribbled down his number for me.

"Sure, I'll call you tonight," I said loudly.

Chapter 15

Lunchtime brought the moment I'd been dreading: the introduction of the candidates at a special rally. We didn't have to make a real speech—that came at the election itself on Friday. We just had to say hi and introduce ourselves, but I wasn't looking forward to getting up in front of the whole school.

"Would the candidates for sophomore class president come up onstage, please," Rich, the commissioner of spirit, announced.

Roni pushed in front of me to get up onstage. It was only when we were up there that we realized we weren't alone.

"What's he doing here?" Roni whispered, before she remembered that she wasn't speaking to me.

I shrugged and grinned before I remembered that I wasn't speaking to her.

Owen was standing beside us, wearing a dark suit, with his hair slicked down and parted to one side.

"And our first candidate is?" Rich said, handing the mike to Owen.

"Good afternoon, everyone . . . is it afternoon? Let me see, yes, it has just turned twelve noon, so good afternoon is correct." Giggles from the audience. "I'd like to introduce myself. My name is Owen Christopher Malcolm Henderson, and I think I will bring dignity and common sense to the office of president. If you vote for me, you won't be disappointed. Thank you."

Polite applause and some sarcastic hoots. Rich handed the mike to Roni.

"Hi, everybody," she yelled, just like a Miss America candidate. "My name is Roni Ruiz and I think I'll make a great soph class president!"

She got loud applause. She handed the mike to me.

"Hi," I said, trying to smile confidently. "My name is . . . crackle, crackle, crackle." I shook the mike and tried again, but it made even louder noises this time. Rich took it, hit it a couple of times, blew into it, and then shrugged. "Sorry, faulty equipment. You'll have to yell."

"My name is Ginger Hartman," I began. I

sounded like a mouse squeaking in a large auditorium. "And I think that I'll—"

"Ginger! Roni! What are you doing onstage?" a voice yelled, twenty times louder than mine. Everyone turned to see where the noise was coming from. The crowd parted dramatically as Justine pushed her way through. "I couldn't wait another minute. I had to tell you the great news," she screamed. "I don't have to go! It's all been canceled. I'm staying here!"

"Justine, that's incredible!" Roni yelled.

Rich turned to the audience and shrugged. "Well, folks, I guess the big news of the day is that Justine is back."

Everyone cheered, even if they didn't know Justine.

Rich tried to go on talking, but the mike was still crackling, so he just waved at the band, who struck up a lively march. Karen fought her way through the crowd to get to Roni, Justine, and me.

"It's a miracle," she yelled. "How did you get out of going to England?"

"It *was* a miracle," Justine said. "Christine started getting cold feet when my dad couldn't find her a house with central heating. And my dad was having all sorts of problems with this English company. Another company offered to buy it and he said okay—it was more trouble than it was worth if his wife and daughter weren't happy. So he's coming home and we're not going and I won't have to wear the red uniform after all. And everything can be the way it was before!"

"Not exactly," Roni and I said at the same moment.

"What do you mean?" Justine asked, looking confused.

"They're having a fight," Karen told her. "They're both running for class president."

"So?" Justine looked puzzled. "Why would that make you enemies? If I'd been here I might have run too, and knowing how popular I am, I think I might just have . . . uh, left both of you in the dust. But I wouldn't expect my friends to hate me for being more successful than they were."

"It's more than that, Justine," I said. "Roni's been playing some dirty tricks on me."

"Like what?"

"Like sneaking in over the weekend to hang posters, and stealing my ideas, *and* stealing my cousin," I said. "And tampering with the mike."

"What?" Roni yelled.

"Oh, come on, Roni," I said. "The mike was working just fine for you and Owen. Then you hand it to me and suddenly it won't work. What did you do, pull the cord loose?"

"Why would I do something like that? I don't need tricks to score points over you."

"Stop it, you two," Justine said. "I was so excited about coming back and you're spoiling it. I don't like seeing my friends like this."

"Me neither," Karen said. "Why don't you two make up?"

"Yeah, go on," Justine agreed. "Be happy that we're all back together and make up, for my sake and for Karen's."

"Sure. If she apologizes to me," I said.

"Me apologize? I've got nothing to apologize for."

Justine took Karen's arm. "Come on, Karen. We'll leave them alone until they can make up. At least you and I can have a good time together."

They began to walk away. Then suddenly Karen stopped dead in her tracks. "Oh, no, it's him again."

"Who?" Justine looked around curiously.

"My nerd. Jeremy. Everywhere I go, he haunts me."

"*That's* your nerd?" Justine asked as she watched Jeremy coming through the crowd beside Owen. "But he's kind of cute, Karen."

"Cute? You think Jeremy is cute?"

"In a sort of nerdy way, I suppose," Justine said. "But he's got gorgeous dark eyes. He looks like a romantic poet, don't you think?"

186

"Well, he did write me that song, and I have to admit that it wasn't bad," Karen agreed. "Maybe he *is* a romantic poet. But I still don't want him to be romantic to me."

"Why don't you introduce us?" Justine said, pulling a reluctant Karen through the crowd. "Maybe I can help keep him away from you. . . ."

We watched them go, our mouths open in shock. Justine was actually seeking out a nerd. I had never thought it was possible.

"It's all your fault," Roni said, bringing me back to reality. "You've split up our friendship."

"My fault? I'm the one person around here who has done nothing wrong."

"Hey, girls, nice presentation," Josh said, coming up between us and putting an arm around each of our shoulders.

"Hers was. The mike stopped working for me," I said.

"Doesn't matter. Everyone got to see you and that's what counts." He was smiling at me. "And what really matters is the speech."

I smiled back at him. "I'm counting on you to help me with that," I said. "Any night this week that you're free, Josh. . . ."

"You're lucky her boyfriend is super busy with the

football team right now," Roni said. "He's the jealous type, you know."

"Roni, would you knock it off," I hissed, pulling Josh away from her.

"She's such a kidder," I said to Josh with what I hoped was a carefree laugh. "Um, what day would be good for you?"

"Any day," he said. "Give me a call when you get home, okay?"

"Sure," I said.

I shot Roni a triumphant smile as he walked away. She was so mad, I could almost see steam coming out of her ears.

That'll show you, Roni Ruiz, I thought. *I can beat you in an election, and I can get the guy you like.*

But as Roni stormed away, I didn't feel so triumphant after all. I'd lost my best friend and I was losing my boyfriend and my other friends too. I'd even lost my cousin! Maybe I hadn't liked her very much, but I never expected her to turn traitor on me!

I hated what was happening. *But none of it is my fault,* I thought. *Everyone else is being mean.* At least Josh was on my side. I would call him tonight. Maybe my life was destined to go in a whole new direction. Maybe I'd be president and hang out with all the popular kids and not even notice that Roni wasn't around or that Ben didn't have time for me. All day long I thought about how different my life would be once I became class president.

After school I headed for the bus stop alone. I was halfway across the parking lot when I noticed Lacey standing behind a clump of palm trees. It almost looked like she was hiding. Suddenly she sprinted across the parking lot, just as a truck pulled up to the gate. She climbed into my boyfriend's pickup, and they sped away together.

"Okay," I said to myself. "So that's how it is. They've been trying to pretend that nothing's going on, but now I've seen it with my own eyes. My innocent little cousin from the boonies went after my boyfriend in a big way and she got him."

Now there was nothing to stop me from going after Josh.

I called him as soon as I got home.

"Ginger, hi!" He sounded glad to hear my voice.

"You told me to call you," I said. "When do you want to get together and work on stuff?"

"I'm baby-sitting my little brothers right now," he said. "Which means I'm kind of trapped for tonight. Do you have little brothers? What a pain."

"I have big brothers," I said. "Equal pain."

"At least you aren't stuck baby-sitting them all the

time," he said. "But I can do some more posters for you tonight, if you'd like. I told you about my graphics program. Do you have any ideas you'd like to see?"

I suggested, "Ginger's got what it takes."

"I like it," he said, "and it's true."

"What is?"

"That you've got what it takes," he said. There was something in his voice that made me think he was talking about more than the election.

"I really appreciate your help, Josh," I said, "and all your encouragement. I'd never have had the nerve to try this if it hadn't been for you."

"My pleasure," he said. "Of course, I'll expect special favors when you make it to the White House."

He laughed again. *Such a friendly, warm laugh,* I thought.

When we finally hung up, I realized that we'd been talking for almost an hour. We'd also arranged to meet after school tomorrow to work on my speech. I had never felt so comfortable with a boy before, except Ben.

I made a decision. I was going to spend the rest of the evening making cookies with my name on them to hand out at school. It was Roni's idea, but she had cheated on the posters and the mike.

All was fair in love, war, and elections!

Chapter

16

I got to school really early the next day, and I took my box of cookies to the front steps. I'm not the world's best cook, so the ones I baked ended up too burned to eat. But I had bought a big box of Oreos and written VOTE GINGER on them in white frosting.

"Hi," I said as each kid came in. "I'm Ginger Hartman. I'm running for soph president. I hope you'll vote for me."

I'd handed out a dozen or so when Roni showed up.

"What do you think you're doing?" she demanded, her eyes nearly bulging out of her head.

"Handing out cookies. Would you like one?"

"You stole my idea!" she said. "I brought cookies today too."

"Great. Now we can both hand them out."

"But it was *my* idea. You stole my idea!"

"The same way you stole my slogans for your posters."

"I did not!"

"Then explain how you had that one about Roni will make your voice heard—exactly the same words as mine! And what a strange coincidence that Lacey went running over to your house right after working on my posters."

"I guess great minds must think alike."

"Aha. At least you agree that I have a great mind."

"I haven't got time to stand here chatting," she said. "I have to get to work with my cookies, which, incidentally, are home baked and look a lot more professional than yours."

She put down her backpack and got out a big cookie tin filled with chocolate cookies that had Roni's name written on them in pink frosting. Okay, so they did look better than mine.

"Hi," she said to the next kid who came in. "I'm Roni. I hope you'll vote for me on Friday."

"I'm Ginger," I said even louder, thrusting my cookie at the unsuspecting person. "I'd like you to vote for *me*."

"Thanks for the cookies," the guy said, "but I'm

a junior. I can't vote for your class."

"I bet you didn't bake them," I growled as he moved off. "They don't look burnt like your normal cookies."

"So my mom helped me."

"That's not fair. I don't have a mother to help me."

"So what do you want me to do? Give away the election because you don't have a mother?"

"I just think it's an unfair advantage that you know I haven't got."

She gave me a withering stare. "I could easily argue that it's unfair to me because English isn't my first language and I have to give a speech in it."

"That's dumb. You've been speaking English almost all your life."

"And you've been without a mother almost all your life. We've both had time to adjust," she said triumphantly. She broke off as another group of kids arrived. "Here, would you like a cookie? I'm Roni and I'd like your vote."

"I'm Ginger, vote for me." I thrust my cookies in front of Roni's cookies.

The kids gave us funny looks.

"Uh . . . no thanks, we're on a diet," one of the girls said.

"See, you're spoiling my chances," Roni snapped.

"Nobody wants a cookie while you're around."

"Maybe because they can tell your cookies are bad."

"Are you saying my mother bakes bad cookies?"

I shrugged. "I was handing them out just fine until you got here."

"Then one of us should move."

"Not me. I was here first."

"It was my idea first."

"Well, I'm not moving."

"Neither am I."

We leaped forward with our cookies again, but all the kids hurried past us.

"Would you go away!" Roni hissed at me.

"No, you."

"I'm not moving."

"Neither am I."

"But you're standing on the right side. Most kids are right-handed. That gives you an unfair advantage."

"Okay, so we'll trade. Does that make you feel better?" I leaped forward and handed a cookie to a couple of girls as they started up the steps, getting to them before they drew level with Roni.

"That's cheating," Roni said. She ran down the steps to join me. I stepped forward even further.

Roni grabbed my shirt and jerked me back. I stumbled against the step, lost my grip, and fell. The cookies went flying.

"Look what you did!" I yelled as I watched my hours of work bouncing down the steps among all the feet. "Do you know how long I spent on those?"

"About three seconds, judging by the sloppy writing."

"At least they don't crumble as much as yours will when they hit the steps."

"Mine aren't going to."

"Wanna bet?" I shook her arm and the tin clattered down the steps, spilling cookies in all directions.

"My cookies!" Roni screamed. "How could you?"

She knelt down and tried to retrieve them.

"Nobody will want them now—they're dirty," I yelled, but she didn't stop. It was getting close to the first bell. More and more students were pouring in through the gates and hurrying up the steps. Some of them didn't even stop to see the mess of cookies. They just ran right over them, crunching them into black and brown crumbs.

"You wrecked my cookies," Roni moaned, still trying to save some.

"You wrecked mine first!"

"Ladies, what's going on here?" a deep voice asked. We looked up to see the tall shape of Principal Lazarow towering over us.

"We were handing out cookies for our election," I mumbled.

"Do you think that littering the steps is a good way to get elected?" Principal Lazarow asked.

"No, sir. That was an accident," Roni said.

"I suggest you ladies run straight to the janitor's closet and borrow a broom to get this cleaned up as quickly as possible," said the principal. "And next time you decide to hand out election favors, either get a better grip on them or choose something less messy."

Roni glared at me as we ran to the janitor's closet.

"Now look what you've done," she said as the bell sounded and we were left alone on the front steps.

"Me? You knocked my cookies over first."

"You brought them when they were my idea."

"You stole my poster idea and made the mike not work."

"You . . . you . . ." Roni's lip quivered a bit and she couldn't finish her sentence. I could tell she was trying not to laugh.

I couldn't help smiling. "This is a pretty impressive mess," I pointed out.

"Very impressive," she agreed, a smile twitching across her face.

"I bet no presidential candidate ever made this big a mess before."

"Only in Washington, maybe."

We both began laughing.

Roni was shaking her head. "Ginger, how did all this start?"

"All what?"

"This dumb fight?"

"I don't remember," I said.

"Me neither."

There was a long pause. Roni attacked the cookie crumbs with her broom. "It is kind of dumb to spoil all these years of friendship over something we don't even remember."

"I guess it is."

"I really hate this."

"Me too."

"And I miss you."

"Me too."

She looked at me. "You are a total idiot, you know."

"Not as big an idiot as you."

"I know that."

I met her eyes for the first time. They were bright

with tears. "Oh, Roni," I said, and I threw my arms around her in a fierce hug. Nothing ever felt so good in my whole life.

"I really don't care if you get elected," she said in a choked voice.

"I don't care either."

"It's just that I was feeling bad about not getting that part."

"And I was feeling bad about losing Ben."

"You're not losing Ben," Roni gasped. "Don't be crazy! He's just super busy."

"I am losing him. He's been disappearing with Lacey when he doesn't have time for me."

"Maybe there's a perfectly good explanation for that."

"Like what?"

"Like . . . something perfectly harmless that I can't actually think of right now."

"See?"

"I'm positive that you don't need to worry, Ginger."

"Maybe I've been dating one guy long enough. Maybe it's not healthy to cling to the same boyfriend for so long. I mean, I'm only a sophomore. I should be dating other guys."

"Like Josh?"

"Maybe."

"Do you really like him?"

"He's funny and nice," I admitted. "Yeah, I guess I do like him."

"Then go for it."

"Are you sure?"

"I can't stop a guy from liking you better than me, can I?" she said. "And I can't stop you from moving on from Ben."

"Roni, you really are a friend. I almost hope you do get elected. I hate getting up in front of people."

"Then withdraw," she teased.

"Never! I have to learn self-confidence someday!"

"Then may the best person win," Roni said. And that I could agree to!

Chapter

17

That afternoon I met Josh after school. We sat on one of the benches in the shade and got a good start on my speech. Well, he got a good start, at least. I just sat there and said, "That's good. I like that," at intervals. He knew exactly what to say—the jokes, the promises. As he was working it occurred to me that I really might win with this speech. It was a strange thought. I wasn't even sure that I truly wanted to be class president. Was I really a dynamic person who could make a difference? I didn't think so. For that you needed someone like Roni.

Josh and I worked together for about an hour. "I gotta go," he said, looking at his watch.

"I really appreciate this, Josh," I said.

"We can finish the speech tomorrow," he said, "and then you'll need some coaching in delivery."

"You want me to be a mail carrier or a stork?"

He laughed. "You sell yourself short too often, Ginger," he said. "You've let me do most of the writing. You say you're not funny, but you are. You just have to believe in yourself."

"You make me feel great, Josh," I said. "Would you let me treat you to pizza tomorrow? Then we could work on the speech in air-conditioned comfort."

"That would be great. This bench is pretty hard, and I never say no to pizza or a cute girl." He got up and started to gather his things. "I'll see you tomorrow, Ginger," he said, and he lightly touched my shoulder before he walked off. It was the first time he had touched me.

I had mixed feelings about that. It made me think I was right all along—Josh was interested in me as well as in my campaign. But it also made me wonder whether I was doing the right thing by taking that next step and getting pizza with him.

Then I reminded myself that I'd spoken to Ben for about ten minutes since school started. And, even though it hurt, I made myself think of Lacey sneaking into Ben's truck after school. I had to admit that it was over and get on with my life.

Still, I hadn't counted on seeing Ben on the way to the pizza parlor Wednesday. Josh and I had agreed to meet at five. He only lived ten minutes from school, so he could go home for a while and then meet me. But there was no way I could have gone home and then come all the way back into the city again on the bus. So I had hung around school, doing my homework. I'd also changed into a new shirt in the girls' locker room and done my hair and makeup before heading out to meet Josh—and my destiny.

That was when I saw Ben coming off the football field. He was walking slowly, with his head down, as if every step was too much for him. He didn't look up until I was almost past him.

I'd made up my mind not to say anything, but he must have sensed it was me. He looked up. "Hi, Gin! What are you doing around campus this late?"

"I'm, uh, meeting a friend to work on my campaign speech," I said. It should have been a moment of triumph. I should have admitted that I was meeting Josh and that we were going for pizza together. After all, I had planned to get Ben jealous. But Ben looked so completely exhausted and miserable that I longed to put my arms around him.

"Tough practice, huh?" I asked gently.

He nodded. "You can say that again. The coach wants miracles. He thinks he can turn me into a star by yelling at me. But he wants me to do the impossible. I'm not another Jerry Rice, Ginger. I never will be."

"You can only do your best, Ben," I said. "I think you're great."

He smiled, a tired sort of smile. "At least I've still got one fan," he said. "I'm just scared that by game day, I'll be too tired and sore to even move."

Suddenly his eyes became more alert. He looked as if he'd just remembered something. "You *are* coming to the game on Friday, aren't you?" he asked.

"This Friday? Isn't it just another scrimmage?"

"Sure, but . . . but . . . I'd really like you to be there. It means a lot to me." He was talking quickly, as though he expected me not to believe him.

"Are you sure you wouldn't rather have Lacey there?" I asked coldly.

He looked puzzled. "Lacey? Why would I want her there?"

"You two seem to be seeing a lot of each other lately. You have lots of little errands to run and things to show each other."

"Oh, that." He smiled. "I'd rather have you there," he said. "In fact, it's very important to me to have you there, Ginger. Will you come?"

"I guess," I said.

A big smile spread across his face. "Great," he breathed.

I glanced at my watch. Any second now Josh would be pedaling up the street to meet me. "I have to go," I said.

Ben nodded. "And I have to see if my feet will make it as far as the locker room. See you Friday, if not before."

"Sure, Ben. See you Friday."

I watched him make his weary way into the locker room. Then I ran to meet Josh.

"This is good pizza," Josh said, pulling out a slice that stretched in a cheesy line across the table before breaking. "Interesting combinations. Look! You can even have potato-and-pineapple pizza."

"If you're into *P*s in a big way," I said. "And don't forget pepperoni."

He laughed. "Potato, pineapple, and pepperoni— I think we've got a winning combination there. Like we've got a winning combination with you and me, Ginger."

I couldn't have scripted the scene better myself. So why were alarm bells sounding in my head? "I just hope I can be the kind of president you think I will,"

I said. "I'm having serious second thoughts about this, Josh. I've never been a leader in my life."

"But you've got what it takes," he said. "You fought like crazy to stop them from paving over your favorite mountain. You fought for something that was important to you. I like that quality, Ginger." He glanced at me and smiled. "There's a lot I like about you. I'm really glad you invited me for pizza. I wanted to ask you out, but I didn't want you to get the wrong impression."

"About what?"

"That I was only helping you with your campaign because I wanted to get to know you better."

"And are you?"

His eyes flirted with me. "First and foremost, I want to make sure that our class has solid leadership," he said grandly. "The quality time spent alone with you is just a fringe benefit."

"If I run, I'm going to have to eliminate corruption from government," I said. "That means no more fringe benefits."

"Say it isn't true," he cried, pretending to be devastated. "But you will still need long, private consultations with your treasurer, won't you?"

"Definitely," I said. "And they will probably need to be over pizza at our favorite pizza parlor."

"My kind of politician," he said. "My kind of girl, in fact."

I could feel his leg brushing against mine under the table and I knew it wasn't by accident. He was looking at me in a way that made me nervous.

This should have been my big moment, when I paid back Lacey and Ben. But there was a picture I couldn't seem to get out of my mind—Ben walking toward the locker room, head down, with his helmet hanging from one hand.

He chose football over me, I told myself. *He chose to spend time with Lacey and the team* and *the cheerleaders.* So why couldn't I get him out of my mind? Why did I long to take him in my arms and hug him fiercely and tell him everything was going to be all right?

"So what do you say, Ginger?" Josh asked. He drew his finger along the back of my hand and up my bare arm. I waited to feel sparks flying across the table, but they didn't. If it had been Ben looking at me like that, I would have melted into jelly by now.

"About what?"

"You know what. About you and me."

"I really like you, Josh," I began.

He made a face. "That doesn't sound like a good beginning. It sounds like, 'I really like you, but get lost.'"

"I really like you and I don't want you to get lost," I said. "You'd be the kind of boyfriend I'd love to have."

"But?"

"But I already have a boyfriend."

"Ben whatshisname? I was asking about him. They said you two were never very serious—more like old family friends."

"That's true," I said. "Ben was always like a big brother to me."

"There you are. He can still be a big brother," Josh said.

"But I don't think of him like a big brother anymore, Josh," I explained. "He's very special to me. I know maybe he doesn't deserve me right now, but I can't stop loving him until I know that it's definitely over."

"So there's still hope, isn't there?" he asked. "If you finally break up with good old Ben, you wouldn't tell me to get lost then?"

"Like I said, I don't want you to get lost now," I said. "Being friends isn't bad, is it?"

He looked at me long and hard. Then he nodded. "Being friends is good," he said. "Friends last longer than dates."

I took a deep breath. "And I'll tell you a secret," I

said. "I know someone who is just dying to get to know you better. She's unattached right now, and she's a really fun person."

"Who?"

"My friend Roni."

"Roni? The one who's running against you?"

I nodded. "That's the one. She only wanted to run for pres so that she could get to meet you."

"Seriously? Wow—how flattering."

"See?" I said. "Not only am I a great president, I'm also a brilliant matchmaker."

"I'll always have a special spot in my heart for you, Ginger," he said.

"And me for you," I said. "Who knows? Maybe we'll wind up going to the senior prom together."

"If Roni will let me," he quipped.

"Shut up!" I laughed.

"So how come she can run against you and still be your friend?" he asked. "I got the feeling you two weren't even speaking to each other."

"We decided that our friendship was more important than being class president. I'll support her if she wins and she'll support me."

He looked at me steadily. "You really are a special girl. I knew my judgment wasn't wrong when I decided I wanted to get to know you better."

"Now, about that speech," I said.

"Oh, the speech—I almost forgot. I suppose we ought to get to work on that. Now that I'm getting perks like pizza, I have to make sure my candidate wins, don't I?"

He pulled out his yellow pad. "Okay. The greatest presidential speech of all time, coming right up."

"Including the Gettysburg Address?"

"The second-greatest presidential speech of all time, coming right up," he corrected smoothly.

I watched his dark head bending over the paper as he wrote. He was funny and nice and confident all at the same time. That was a pretty special combination. Most boys I knew were either nice but dorky, or popular and confident but also conceited. There weren't many like Josh White. And I was going to set him up with Roni.

It just goes to show what a terrific best friend I am, I thought with a smile.

Chapter

18

By lunchtime on Friday, I had a truly killer speech. I had practiced it in front of the mirror for hours, and even I had to admit I was pretty good. I went through my usual panic attack when I looked out over that crowd at the rally, but I caught Josh's eye and he winked at me.

"I'm doing this for him," I whispered, and after that my voice didn't even tremble. Well, only a little at the beginning.

Roni's speech was also good. She made the whole audience howl with laughter. Owen's speech was . . . well, Owenish. Weird and nerdlike. He promised more computer labs and a sci-fi convention held on campus each year.

"I thought you were great," Roni said as we left the stage. "I bet you win."

"I thought you were great too," I said. "And you were funny. People like to laugh. I wouldn't be surprised if you won."

"We'll just have to wait until they count the votes, won't we?" she said.

"I guess we will," I answered. "Do you want to come to the football game tonight with me? I promised Ben I'd go. And maybe we can get Karen and Justine to come too, now that you and I are finally talking again."

"Sorry, but I've got something else planned."

"Like what?"

"Oh, just some kids who want me to get together with them. Nothing special."

"Oh," I said. I felt as though the air had been knocked out of me. Roni had never gotten together with kids who hadn't invited me too. Why hadn't Roni asked if she could bring me along? Suddenly I wondered if Karen and Justine were also going to be there. I'd hardly seen them all week.

Roni wouldn't even look at me, and I couldn't think of a thing to say to her. Maybe I had been wrong to think our big fight hadn't changed our friendship. Maybe we wouldn't be as close as before.

Roni glanced at the door the student council members had disappeared through. They were tabulating the votes while we waited. "I guess they have to check and double check," Roni muttered.

"Not the ones I paid off," I quipped. "They just put them all in my pile."

Roni managed to laugh. "I won't really mind too much if you win," she said. "I mean, it would be time consuming, and I'm signing up for debate team."

"Go for it," I said. "But you could handle both. You're the sort of person who can do anything she wants. I would be surprised if you don't win. Everyone likes you."

"They like you too."

"By the way," I said. "I told Josh that you liked him."

"Ginger, you didn't! What did he say?"

"He seemed kind of interested."

"But what about you?"

"I told him I already had a guy."

"Thanks. I owe you one."

"You could concede."

"Don't push it," she said, laughing. I felt a little better.

The noise level dropped as the commissioner of elections came out onstage. "The votes have been counted," she said, "and the results are as follows: Ginger Hartman, one hundred and fifty-three votes."

There were cheers.

Okay, so I'd lost badly. They did like Roni better after all. I set my face into a polite smile.

"Roni Ruiz, one hundred and sixty-one votes."

More cheers.

Roni looked at me and I looked at Roni. The awful truth had just dawned on us.

"Owen Henderson, six hundred and twelve votes."

There was very sparse, polite applause.

Owen came up onstage holding up his hands in V-for-victory signs. It was one of the oddest moments of my life. I didn't know whether to laugh or cry.

"It can't be right," Roni blurted. "They counted wrong. They had someone nearsighted reading the votes. They mistook Roni for Owen."

"I'm in shock," I agreed as kids began to crowd around us.

"Sorry, Ginger," a girl from my math class said. "I wanted to vote for you, but I couldn't vote against Roni."

"Knowing how close you two were," someone else added, "I just couldn't do it. I didn't want to split up your friendship forever. . . . I just couldn't choose between you. . . ." The excuses were coming thick and fast. Owen was still dancing around onstage, even though the entire crowd was gathered around us.

Roni and I looked at each other and grinned. "Our classmates knew better than we did," she said. "They realized our friendship is pretty special and that something like this could destroy it."

"And you know what else?" I added. "All those people who were willing to doom the class to a year of Owen must definitely like us a lot!"

Chapter

19

That evening I sat all alone in the bleachers and watched Ben's football game. It wasn't much fun with nobody to talk to. I remembered how we'd all gone to games together last year and Roni had nearly fallen off the bleachers because she used to yell and dance around so much. Would we ever get back to the way we were? Now that Karen and Justine were at school again, there was nothing to stop us from having fun and getting back to our old lifestyle. So why weren't we doing it? I had barely even seen Karen and Justine this week, and they'd both said they had plans tonight. Was it possible that they didn't like me anymore? *Some election day this was,* I thought, *and some dumb birthday.* Not a single one of my friends had even remembered to give me a card. My supposed boyfriend had been too busy running around with a football to think of me.

The game ended and Ben came over.

"I hope you're not going to tell me to find my own ride home again," I said.

"Of course not," he said. "After I made you come, the least I can do is run you home."

The very least, I thought angrily. *You could have offered to take me out somewhere special.*

"I'm totally exhausted," he said, as if he could read my thoughts. "I just want to crawl into bed and sleep forever."

"You did great in the game," I said.

He nodded. "Yeah, I wasn't too bad, was I? Maybe all that yelling is paying off."

I waited for Ben to get showered and changed and then we drove home in his truck. I was still fighting back disappointment. He could have taken me out for ice cream or a soda, couldn't he? Even if he was super tired, it wouldn't have been too much. He hadn't even mentioned my birthday. I had no idea whether I should remind him or not. If he really cared about me, he would have done something special, wouldn't he? I bet Josh would have remembered.

We pulled up outside my house. It was in total darkness. That meant Todd and my dad were out for the evening.

"Here we are," Ben said. "Would you like me to wait to see that you get safely inside?"

"You're not coming in?"

"I think I should get straight home," he said. "I need to soak in a long hot bath and then get some sleep. But I'll call you tomorrow, Ginger. Maybe we can do something this weekend, okay?"

"Okay," I said flatly. I didn't even look at him as I climbed out of the truck. Ben didn't care about me at all.

I walked up the front path and turned my key in the lock. *I will not cry,* I thought over and over, *I will not cry.*

I flicked on the light and slammed the door behind me. The whole living room was full of balloons and streamers. A huge banner saying HAPPY BIRTHDAY, GINGER! was stretched across the back wall. The table was laden with food and presents.

"What . . . ?" I stammered.

"Surprise!"

People leaped out from behind sofas and chairs and doors. I put my hands to my face and burst into tears.

"Did we fool you?" Ben asked gently, coming up to put his arms around me.

"You guys," I sobbed. "I totally didn't expect . . ."

"You must have done a good job, Ben," Roni said.

"I thought I was pretty good," Ben replied. "You should have seen her face when I said I was going straight home to take a bath."

I was laughing and crying at the same time. So were all my friends. They crowded around me, Roni and Karen and Justine and Josh and Lacey and Ben and Todd and half of the sophomore class.

"How did you manage to do all this?" I stammered. "You and I weren't even talking, Roni."

"Blame Lacey," Roni said. "It was all her idea."

I looked at Lacey and she blushed bright red. "I wanted to thank you for being so nice to me, Cuz. You took all that time and trouble to make sure I settled in at school and I sure appreciated it. I wanted to do something really special for you. So I got together with Roni and Ben and we planned this out. Ben was wonderful. I had to keep bugging him about driving me places, because I'm still not too good with the buses."

"So that's what you were doing," I said, brushing away tears.

"I felt bad that I couldn't tell you," Lacey said, dropping her voice and leaning close to me. "But I can tell you one thing. You don't have to worry about your boyfriend—all he did the whole time was talk about you." She grinned.

I turned to Ben and wrapped my arms around his neck. "Thank you," I whispered. "You're a great guy, you know that? I'm lucky to have you."

"We're lucky to have each other," he whispered back. Then he kissed me gently, even though everyone in the room was making dumb noises and laughing at us.

Josh tapped my shoulder. "Okay, enough of that. Ginger, I'm still waiting."

"For what?" Ben asked suspiciously.

"For an official introduction."

I grabbed Roni's arm. "Roni—Josh. Josh—Roni. The rest is up to you guys. I'm the birthday girl, I don't have to work."

Everyone started attacking the food. Karen and Justine brought me a plate.

"She wanted me to invite Jeremy," Karen said, giving Justine a despairing look. "But I knew you wouldn't want nerds at your party."

"You could just have invited Jeremy without the nerd pack," Justine said. "How am I going to get to know him better if I never get a chance to be in a romantic setting with him?"

"You can't seriously still like him, now that you've seen his friends," Karen said, rolling her eyes.

"Don't ask me why I like him. I just do," Justine said. "It was like magic, our eyes meeting across a crowded room."

"Unbelievable," Karen said.

"What is?" Roni asked, squeezing in to join us.

"That Justine likes my nerd."

"It just proves one thing," I said. "That there is the right boy out there for everyone—"

"And it only takes a Boyfriend Club to bring them together," we all said at once.